"*Still Life* is a stunning novel about the power of art, the complexity of relationships, and the transfiguration of cast offs, all seen through the recomposition of a broken life. Skenazy writes with mysterious clarity and extraordinary compression; the novel shimmers with intelligence and grace."

Elizabeth McKenzie
author of *The Portable Veblen*

"*Still Life* offers a rare and beautiful story about the power of our own will to address the disconnects in our lives. After the loss of his wife, Will Moran steps out of family routines and social norms to paint rocks. It's a novel of voyaging while staying in place, keeping house while refusing all chores, opening hearts while closing doors, and squeezing meaning from stones."

Thad Nodine
author of *Touch and Go*

"Like a captivating still life, Skenazy's novel renders perspectives and relationships with nuance and depth. Hypnotic writing, surprising characters, and searching reflections on art and meaning pulse through a moving story about the visible and invisible sediments of longing and fidelity."

Henry Martin
author of *Agnes Martin: Pioneer, Painter, Icon*

STILL LIFE

PAUL SKENAZY

Cover illustration copyright © 2021 by Janet Fine

Author photograph by Shelby Graham

Published by Paper Angel Press
paperangelpress.com

ISBN 978-1-953469-49-6 (Trade Paperback)

10 9 8 7 6 5 4 3 2 1

FIRST EDITION

To Jason, Sarah, and Matt

If a thing is worth doing once,
it is worth doing over and over again.

Mark Rothko

1

WHEN HIS WIFE, EDIE, DIED, Will Moran closed his front door and began to paint pictures of rocks. Rocks and bottles, plastic shovels and pails, driftwood and bunched-up rags. Drawings first—in pencil and charcoal. Then he moved to temperas, oils, and acrylics. He advanced from paper to cardboard, cardboard to canvas and Masonite. Day after day, he devoted himself to painting, rocks, and his walks.

·   ·   ·

Edie and Will met in 1978, when Will got a job teaching history at Santa Cruz High. It wasn't love at first sight so much as bored faces at the fall staff meeting, the two trading looks as they lamented the thirty-five minutes it took the principal to explain how to deal with attendance problems and late homework.

"I think you checked your watch more times than I did, and I stopped counting my glances at twenty," was the way Edie introduced herself.

"I didn't count, but I suspect you won. I'm new here, need to be careful."

"You're safe as long as you wear socks and show up at football games," she said to him.

"That I can handle. It's the meetings that get me."

"Either they're in their seats or they're absent, they finish the assignment or don't," Edie said. "Is that so hard?"

"Maybe it's different in Santa Cruz? What with the auras and things?"

"You'll stop joking once some Harmony or Rainbow explains that her mother's tarot reading warned her not to come to school for a week."

He laughed.

"I've got two Willows, a Blossom, and a Charity; no Rainbows or Harmonys. In Tomales Bay where I taught, the favorites were Phoenix for boys and Heather for girls."

"I'm headed back to my classroom to have a heart-to-heart with Karma right now," she said to him.

"I'm so sorry."

"You'll be sorrier when you hear the same speech next fall," she answered, turning away down the hall.

The next day he found chocolate chip cookies in his mailbox:

I'm Edie. I teach English, like jazz, art, and
foreign films, and have a seven-year-old
daughter named Helen who helped me bake
these. My husband died three years ago and I am
not looking for a replacement. Helen says to tell

you to invite me to lunch, but I decided I'd rather ask you. I checked your schedule; you're free. Today? Tomorrow?

He chose Today so he wouldn't have time to get nervous.

They repeated the meeting the next day. They left the teachers' lounge after school, sat on the swings for half an hour before smiling goodbyes to each other. Then two more lunches the next week, the homecoming game that Friday night. She picked him up for a beginning-of-the-year faculty potluck on Saturday. He met Helen when he came to dinner the following Monday.

Wednesday, there were more cookies in his mailbox—this time oatmeal, with a note from Helen: "I made these myself. Thank you for coming to dinner. Mom says she likes you."

It was his turn to bake. He made brownies and left them for Edie: "Why are you and your daughter so shy? How about dinner instead of lunch? Today? Tomorrow?"

Will had never been courted before. He thought of himself as a lone ... not wolf, maybe raccoon, raiding the leftovers. He felt unsure of himself almost anywhere but in class, waiting to spill wine on a rug or show up with his shirt buttoned wrong. "Mr. Fumble," Edie called him with a laugh when he had trouble undoing her bra and untangling his feet from his pants. She didn't mind lending a hand.

•   •   •

Edie and Helen made room for Will in their home, he for them in his heart. Helen moved through grammar, middle, and high school, college at Berkeley, to Minnesota for medical school. She became a pediatrician, fell in love with Amos (another pediatrician) and stayed. Twenty-five years went by. Will and Edie continued to catch each other's eyes at faculty meetings, hold hands at soccer games, and teach English and history. It was Will who first noticed the spots on Edie's arms and legs and insisted she see a doctor. She put it off until the semester ended.

So it was late June 2003 when Edie was diagnosed with lymphoma. She took a year's leave, then extended that to two. Will retired over Edie's objections. He knew Edie would never return to the classroom. He drove her to and from her doctors' appointments. He got her to the emergency room the night she sank into a coma, slept the next three nights in the hospital chair, and put her gently back into her bed at home when the imminent danger passed. After that episode, he hovered over her even more conscientiously, and more tenderly, sensing that the end was near.

Students and friends rallied around. People visited, offering encouragement, a bottle of wine, the latest gossip. Month after month there would be a knock on the front door in the late afternoon. If he got there quickly enough, he would see someone he knew or their child with food in hand. If he were busy seeing to Edie, the food—a homemade casserole, pizza, Thai or Chinese takeout—would be sitting on the front porch, wrapped in a kitchen towel, foil, or on a plastic tray. Three nights a week, rain or shine.

"As dependable as the garbage collectors," Will liked to say.

"Or President Jed Bartlet," Edie would reply.

Edie died in early July, 2005. At the memorial, friends talked of her bravery, how she remained upbeat despite her pain. She lasted longer than many, they told Will by way of consolation.

Helen was there for the last week. After the burial, she took control.

"You look exhausted, Dad. Your vigil is over. It's time to think about your own health. Rest. Let me take care of you for a while."

Will knew rest was impossible. He shuddered when he imagined Helen caring for him, figuring that was something that wouldn't come for a dozen or so years. He was tired. But what tired him most was being the object of attention, sympathy, and kindness. Not that he wanted to be slapped around, he quickly said to himself. But ignored: that might be just the cure for whatever ailed him; whatever could be mended, without Edie in his life.

The food deliveries stopped two weeks after the funeral. Phone calls diminished in a statistically calculable curve. There were cards, emails, notes in the mailbox and messages on the answering machine, but Will ignored them except when Helen insisted.

"These are your friends, Dad. They want to help."

He didn't answer Helen, just stared beyond her at the kitchen wall, where a dark rectangle of bright paint untouched by the sun revealed the spot where a Diebenkorn abstract used to hang. It was already gone to Goodwill, along with most of the other art posters Edie had collected over her years of museum visits. Helen had the energy of ten when it came to housecleaning.

To Will, Helen seemed to deal with grief as if it were an ailment of one of her patients: a childhood earache or persistent cough best treated with an antibiotic, renewed vigor, and impatience. She seemed to enjoy hectoring. He remembered months back, Edie staring at the phone after saying goodbye to her:

"You know, Will, I never get off the phone without Helen leaving me with one nagging issue or another to brood over. Last week it was that the sofa cushions were too soft for my lower back."

"And today?" Will asked.

"It's whether I am wasting sponges when I replace them every week the way I do."

"Important," was all Will could say to that, though he knew the sponges were important. To Edie at least. Every Sunday night since the first week they lived together Will watched Edie throw one away and open its replacement. "Some things in this world don't deserve attention but require it anyway," she used to say. "Memory needs props. Habit's my crutch."

Will fought his own battle with habit those first months after Edie died, when he bought sponges by the dozen and opened one every Sunday night well into November. Or when he realized how he stumbled still over Edie's slippers getting out of bed in the morning—the same pair, in the same spot where Edie used to place them, night after night. A spot where he invariably tripped going to the bathroom to pee, however many years it was they'd been married. Even in her last weeks, Edie insisted the slippers remain where they always had been. By then Edie could no longer rise by herself but would instead ring a tiny bell to wake Will, who would insert her dwindling feet into the worn shoes. And now, Edie gone, Will found himself carefully setting those tired slippers alongside the bed still, where they continued to get in his way.

Will wanted to stop stumbling over the past. He wrote that in one of his first entries in the notebook he started, hoping to learn something from the wild and fitful thoughts that consumed him.

> *Not answering the phone causes more grief than what's said, Helen insists. Goodbye's a sacred word, hello makes the sun come up. But lives go on, me or no me. Or don't go on. No medicine in my flesh. Edie would be the first to confirm that.*

Helen made it her mission to keep Will connected with his old friends. She returned their calls, set up visits for tea or sandwiches late afternoons, sent Will to his closet for a clean shirt as if instructing her children on table manners. She kept after Will to sort through the towels and sheets in the hall closet, the good silverware left from Edie's first marriage, her school papers. She insisted Will participate in her daily phone calls back to St. Paul with husband Amos and their three children, where Will heard about the swarms of mosquitos that had encircled the summer house at the lake. He listened to his grandchildren's reports on swim lessons, the fish they caught, and their new video game.

He would sit mornings at the dining room table, a newspaper propped in front of him, not reading so much as turning pages so Helen might think he was. She kept up a steady conversation with his muteness while she answered condolence cards, thanked people for donations in Edie's name, or wrote long letters in response to notes from Kitty—Edie's lifelong friend, settled for the moment somewhere in Eastern Europe, and dependable as always with a postcard full of information on wherever her wanderings took her.

•   •   •

Sharing the house with Helen, Will discovered that the only place he felt safe was on the roof. *Used to be afraid of heights, wonder why I'm not anymore,* he asked himself in his notebook. *The world is different up there. So am I.* He sat for hours on the rough asphalt shingles, looking off across block on block of TV antennas and through the telephone lines to the horizon, where ocean, air, and fog met. He took solace in the silence, the clouds, the pale greens, browns, and reds of the rooftops. He would often bring a book along, thinking to read, but he rarely did. He would just sit, hour after hour, or as long as he could until Helen persuaded him to examine the contents of a drawer or return a phone call from someone he never liked all that much.

By late July, as Helen readied herself to return to Minnesota, she left Will with enough admonitions to ensure his days would be full and useful. Instead, he retreated to his roof. *No more calls on me,* he wrote. *No one to care for, answer to, worry about. Nothing to do but what I want. And what is that, old fart?*

When the roof lost its magic, Will walked. He left his house late each night and wandered down to the beach. It was two miles as the crow flies, but three or four for Will. He traced no set course, letting impulse direct him. Once on the sand, he would watch from the shadows. He saw people huddled near fires, noisy groups throwing Frisbees into the dark, couples folded into blankets or sleeping bags against the cold, dogs running back and forth with excitement. When he had his fill, he would trudge back home, empty his shoes of the sand, and head for bed. *Stare, wonder, walk. For hours, even days,* he wrote. *Till the legs or heart give out. Or I find something better to do with my time.*

Will had never been very talkative; now he was quieter still. He kept the lights off and the blinds drawn, living in a perpetual twilight breakfast to bedtime. What he needed, he thought, was to be alone. What he needed, he soon discovered, was to collect rocks.

•   •   •

When Will grew up in Los Angeles, his father would take him to the Santa Monica pier. First it was for the merry-go-round, then the Ferris wheel and the rest of the rides. By the time Will could bike there, he'd lost interest in the amusement park. He would walk down the beach, which stretched for miles. He was already a loner, not so much friendless as uninterested in most of the people he knew. He found solace in the sand, the waves, and the chance to stare at the other beachgoers as he trudged along in silence.

It was when Will moved to Tomales Bay that he fell in love with the winter storms. The tamed urban expanses of Southern California gave way to hidden inlets and narrow breaks carved out of steep cliffs. He would clamber down to whatever isolated beach he could find, over rocks made slick by the rain. He'd strip off socks and shoes, roll up his jeans, and spend afternoons walking slowly up and down the sand, collecting pebbles, glass, or whatever else caught his eye. He loved the way each storm redesigned the landscape, depositing whole tree trunks and massive boulders.

It was the same in Santa Cruz. While Edie stomped from one end of a beach to the other, Will inched his way along, bending and crouching. He'd pick up and discard small stones with a random, unthinking impulse. She'd return to him, grab his arm, cajole a longer stride. Then he'd stoop down to examine some small would-be treasure and he was lost to her. He'd weigh his interest in a pebble's shape, the color of a wave-washed glass fragment. He'd stick them in pants pockets, shirt pockets, coat pockets, plastic sandwich bags, and empty them into a basket on his dresser at night, or leave them on paper plates to dry. Sometimes Will forgot to empty his pockets, and the stones would wind up as broken crumbs or fine sand amid the lint or caught in the mesh of his socks. When Edie got fed up, Will would carry his finds to the storage shed, reexamine his treasures for an hour or two, discard some and preserve others. Those that survived ended up amid accumulated clothes, old posters, unused kitchen gadgets—Edie's household rejects in her annual effort to simplify. "Things aren't of use if we're not using them. Either they sit in my hand or they live somewhere else" was the epigram for her spring tear through drawers, shelves, and cabinets. The shed became home to their forgotten selves: what once mattered, once was new, once held interest; what couldn't be trashed, needn't be noticed.

Edie gone, Will took up his beach habits again. He collected as he went, then dropped the night's accumulation in a heap alongside the mail that often sat, unopened, on his hall floor for days. Mornings, he rinsed the pebbles in the kitchen sink, sorted, let them dry, and dropped the stones that remained onto the living room floor, next to the old sofa. He started carrying a backpack with him and began taking home larger and larger rocks and pieces of driftwood, adding these to his pile beside the couch.

One afternoon, Will picked up a pencil, rummaged around for paper, and tried to draw a few rocks that interested him. He tried on and off the rest of the day, and again the next. He found charcoal sticks in the storage shed, but soon finished with those—*Too flaky,* he wrote in his notebook: *Rubs off on hands, face, everywhere but the paper. Rubs me the wrong way.*

He hunted through the shed for the temperas Helen used in high school to paint signs on cardboard. He found an old brush, and went to work with the red, navy blue, and bright green that were the only colors that weren't dried out.

•   •   •

When he tried to write directly about his new habits, Will had little to say. *Looking instead of asking, or trying to find answers,* was how he put it, then crossed that phrase out. He had no interest in hidden meanings. It was enough, he decided, to just be alone, walk the streets, and draw.

When he took the time to glance through his mail— usually the day he took his meager store of garbage and recycling to the curb below his house—he would find a biweekly postcard from Kitty. She'd report on the height of European church steeples, the crowds along the Amsterdam canals, the pleasure of biking through the flat Dutch countryside. Helen called wanting details about how he spent his days.

"Puttering. Cleaning, sorting. You know. Enjoying the chilly, foggy August we're having that keeps the tourists away."

"You sound like a misanthrope, Dad."

He'd nod agreement, and search for an anecdote to satisfy her curiosity: the dog who toppled over in the waves chasing after a stick; a naked toddler being prodded up to the bathrooms by his frantic mother, leaving a trail of pee in his wake.

He heard her gathering breath for a question.

"Tell me about the kids," he'd interject. "Better yet, let me talk to them."

He didn't tell Helen that he seldom left the house until the evening, when a chill hung in the night air. He didn't let her know about his nightly scavenging of discarded children's pails, plastic shovels and castle molds, ballpoint pens and sand-covered tennis balls, or how often he'd fill his backpack with beer cans and folded paper diapers someone forgot to pick up either in haste or negligence. *We've trained dog owners to carry plastic bags,* he wrote. *Why not parents?*

During the day, Will tried to draw the beach pebbles and driftwood he brought home with him. He'd arrange and rearrange the stones—bunched together, with space between, in rows, some leaning on others, larger behind or in front of smaller. He'd try to build the flatter pieces into towers, like the cairns that shaped his steps when he hiked. ("Stone watchtowers," Edie had called them.) But his small souvenirs-turned-still-lifes defeated him. *Why defeated? What battle am I in?* he mocked himself.

> *Surface after surface, no whole. I remember too much: when I got them, where. I'm not painting a family album, just rocks. ('Just'—fucking hard word, demeans as it demands.)*

A desire to find relationships—or what he wanted to imagine as relationships—kept Will drawing and writing notes to himself: *A stone fits another, or doesn't. Accents, removes, maybe hints at something. Or so I pretend. Until rocks tell me otherwise, I need to assume that's my illusion, not the earth's.*

It was late September when Will admitted he was stumped by what he called his *purposeless stones: Are they mine? Are they purposeless? Useless question. Add pencils, pens, paint, brushes, paper. Add color, shape, boundary, shadow: still purposeless?*

9.25

There's no "with" with stones, maybe. Carry one in a pocket, years pass, the stone is worn down a bit by my thumb, it warms in my palm. Is it still only itself, no relation to me? Does art, or keys I carry in the same pocket, do anything to the rock's rockiness?

●   ●   ●

When he wasn't painting, Edie haunted him. He found her everywhere: in the photographs along the hallway; the creak of his bed; the slope of the sofa cushions. He went on a tear, starting with the framed photos. He looked at each in turn as he wrapped it in newspaper—shots of Helen graduating high school, college, then medical school; him and Edie in front of a cathedral, on a beach, or smiling at the rail of an Alaskan cruise ship. He took down his parents' wedding portrait; the photo of Edie's grandparents becoming U.S. citizens, their arms raised for the pledge; the snapshots of his grandchildren doing everything from crawling to riding ponies.

No need to see what I know. If I remember, I remember; if I don't it won't help to walk down the hall and stare at their faces staring at me. I need wall space, empty space, empty time. Need for what? Answer that, old man.

He disconnected the answering machine and unplugged the phone, though it seldom rang except for Helen's twice-a-week check-ins. When a neighbor knocked on his door with a worried message from Helen, he went to a phone booth, called her back, and apologized: "I need some time away from all the ringing." He promised to call her at least once a week. She started to argue, but Will pretended he couldn't understand what she was saying: "Must have a bad connection. I'll call back tomorrow, I promise." And he did, deliberately extending the time between calls. *Sunday. Family day. The phone booth's my church, complete with a sermon from Helen.*

Will got rid of his stereo, the coffee table, the armchair, and the sofa. He moved on to the dining room chairs, the dishes, pots and pans, Persian rugs, and the old radio he kept out in the storage shed. He stripped his house down to a dining room table, his bed and dresser, a mattress on the floor of Helen's old room, wooden packing crates he brought in from the shed to serve as bedside tables for the guests he didn't expect, two benches along the kitchen counter, and a bunch of overstuffed pillows edging what used to be the living room.

"Too many programs," he announced to Luís, the gardener, when he offered him his TV. He remembered the hours he spent watching late into the night, the volume low so as not to wake Edie, as a movie or talk show gave way to someone sweeping up rug samples or rolling their muscular body behind a new workout marvel. *That distraction gone,* he wrote. *Nevermore know who kills, convicts, saves whose languid body, warm smile, enticing hair.*

He liked the thank-you cards he got from Luís's two children: full of vivid colors and designs that would peter out before they took actual shape as an animal or person. He was struggling to make sense of his first how-to art book that explained, in an assured way, that shapes tend to flatten at the edge of paper. So if a painter wanted to create the illusion of roundness, depth, and dimensionality, it was best to center objects. This made no sense to Will. He wasn't sure what he was seeking and his centering did little for his still two-dimensional efforts at reproducing three-dimensional shapes. He tried imitating the children by shifting his focus from the center to the borders: *Will the weight of the stones tip the composition left or right, displace line and color into grams and pounds?*

Once he freed himself from his possessions, he tried the same tactic with time. He'd already said no to Helen's Thanksgiving invitation, trading privacy now for the promise of a long visit next summer. He decided not to go down to L.A. to his brother Jerry's for Christmas, or travel up to Marysville after to see Edie's family as he usually did and as they expected him to continue to do after her death—until his own, he supposed, or theirs. He just wanted to go about his business. He called painting his business by then, along with his walks. *Family love: always afraid I'd lose it. Unnerving now. I don't want offers of guest bedrooms, turkey and stuffing. But don't I want the chance to reject them?*

It was then (October 17 was the entry in his notebook) that he accepted the fact that this was as close as he could get to what he wanted to do: walk, collect stones and driftwood, stare at the rocks and disfigured branches that littered his living room floor, and try to paint them.

> *Figured I'd be done by now, back planting,
> reading, even traveling. Mourning Edie the rest
> of my life in my taciturn way. Turn into a
> granddad. Rejoin ACLU, go to City Council
> meetings, stump for Democrats, volunteer at the
> nursing home until I need to check myself in. But
> the rocks interest me. They are implacable,
> friendly. They never talk back.*

His early Christmas gift to himself was the way Will described the empty months ahead: dark skies, rain storms, beaches filling slowly with more battered pieces of driftwood, scraps of worn glass, and rocks thrown up by the waves. Walks and beach-combing, quiet and painting. By the new year, Will hoped, he'd be able to draw a rock or two with some confidence, as he knew he couldn't yet, his lines and proportions all askew, his colors mismatched. *Though what is not mismatched? What matched to what? Art as outfit coordination? Marriage brokering?* he challenged himself, not expecting an answer.

With the couch gone, Will expanded his rock piles across the width of the living room. *Pads on couches—all three we've had—too meager for my butt,* he confided to his notebook. *Can't complain about that with rocks.*

At first Will drew on a pad of paper, but it was forever shifting under him. He dug around in his shed until he found an old children's easel—green blackboard on one side, white dry erase surface on the other, two large red gutters at the base. He C-clamped large rectangles of cardboard on the easel, plopped himself down in the sagging seat of an old beach chair, and set his temperas around him on the floor. He tried painting larger rocks: *Fewer dangling prepositions to these than my pebbles. Bless my geologic ignorance.*

But the rocks proved as resistant to his artistry as the smaller stones. Out of temperas and out of patience with himself, he put the easel back into the shed and headed for the Tracery, the lone downtown stationery and art store.

•　　•　　•

That's how Jess Arnold reentered Will's life. Will had always thought Jess a pleasant, if forgettable, figure—one of the several thousand students who'd drifted through his classroom over the years. He remembered him as an uninspired boy—medium height, medium brain, medium energy, his face lost amid slumped shoulders and a hooded sweatshirt he wore whatever the weather. He seemed ready to drift through school, comfortable in the shadows while his twin brother Jeff played soccer and had a lead role in every school theater production. He'd been interested in both boys because of their mother Nancy, pregnant with them a decade and a half earlier when she was his student and Edie had taken her on as a project. He knew Jess had gone on to the college in town, but little more about him or his brother. Nancy had resurfaced as one of the organizers of the food brigade that kept Will and Edie in chicken casseroles and mesclun salads. Payback, Will thought to himself when he saw Nancy drop off yet another dinner—her way to thank Edie for helping her navigate her pregnancy and graduate high school. Though she raised the boys herself through their teens, she was now married, he knew, to Dave Cartelli, a successful lawyer with clients all over California.

"Sorry about your wife," Jess said to Will. "Mom told me Mrs. Moran died."

Will switched subjects.

"I didn't know you worked here, Jess. Or worked at all," he added, thinking that Cartelli could afford to cover Jess's college expenses.

"My stepdad's a stickler," Jeff explained. "'You pay your way or you do things my way,' he likes to say. "I'm not a fan of his way."

He stopped there. The boy wants some sympathy or at least curiosity, Will thought to himself. But Will didn't have any to offer, and responded to Jess's disclosure with a noncommittal nod.

Jess steered Will through his purchases: cheap canvases, a palette, tubes of student paint, thinner, gesso, and brushes. Then, walking by a house one night, he noticed a garage sale sign that included art materials in its long list of household items. He bought thirteen canvases, a portable easel, and thirty-five tubes of paint, along with six brushes. He lined up the eleven-by-fourteen canvases on their sides along one wall. Their white edges contrasted nicely with the bumpy dark unevenness of the rocks that by then overran the living room. *Is color a gift to the empty canvas or a theft of its whiteness? My question for the month.*

He moved the round dining room table, resting on its oversized central pedestal, to a position in front of the fireplace in the living room. He covered it with a white sheet and arranged his rocks on top. His models—as he liked to call them—would sit, with variations, for days on end as he shifted among canvases. He took a large tarp from the storage shed and nailed it over the already closed blinds at the front window, then went to the hardware store for three work lights that he clamped at various angles on the fireplace mantle. He had decided that sunlight would interfere with his work.

> *What can interfere with something else? Or what doesn't? Interfere requires direction or desire, a route to or from. It comes down to light: I can't stand the so-called natural version. I want to live among slashes of shadow from my spotlights. Maybe intrude is the right word, not interfere.*

Each day, he dressed in one of four paint-spattered white shirts and a semi-clean pair of increasingly gessoed jeans. The rest of his closet, the clothes still on their hangers, took its place in the shed atop a pile of boxes.

> *If Helen saw my wardrobe, let alone house, she'd move in, serve me cottage cheese sandwiches with canned pineapple chasers the rest of my life. Not much worse, I suppose, than the canned soup and frozen vegetables I make for myself.*

•　　　•　　　•

With the table shrouded in a sheet, Will thought he should be done with its place in his and Edie's life. But he lost whole days to memories: the rushed meals when Helen was in high school, the wine and coffee stains left by his years grading papers. After one dinner party, Edie was up until three a.m. trying to repair a crevice a dinner guest made with his steak knife. Will was sure the gash was there forever. But Edie rubbed and re-rubbed with walnut and sandpaper. "Life's in the grain," Edie liked to repeat. "Never cut against it. Mend what you hurt; repair what you scar."

Mend hurt; repair scar, he wrote one morning, hoping to purge his thoughts of the formula by writing it down.

> *Mends don't last long; scars reveal our efforts to*
> *repair. Get cut enough, all that's left is scar*
> *tissue. I love the cracks in stones. Are they*
> *breaks? Edie told me the Japanese accentuate the*
> *cracks, fill them in bowls and vases with gold.*
> *I've only got paint and ineptitude.*

Nothing seemed to disappear, Will realized. Or everything, he corrected himself. Disappeared, but didn't; stayed, but left, preserved and eroded. He retreated from this conundrum to his paint, shifting around the living room while he looked, as he wrote, *for some point of view that matters:*

> *As if one matters more than another. As if an*
> *ocean has one. But people: forced into each other,*
> *rubbing, one against another. Why—how—*
> *choose one person, one rock? Why put it next to*
> *another, stare at it from right rather than left? I*
> *don't know and don't know how to find out. Why*

this color or that on maps to show countries?
Who gets noticed that way, who forgotten? So
blame mapmakers for wars? Who else?

•   •   •

For two days after that comment, he didn't paint at all. He moved his easel in an arc around the dining room table, adjusted the legs up and down, from knee height to full extension, dissatisfied with each angle he created. *How can I figure out my position in the living room, let alone world?* he asked himself.

He decided to be systematic. He'd create a five-day circuit around his still life each week, allowing himself two wild cards when whim took over. He got out a compass, drew a circle on the back of a drawing, ruled out hexagons around the edges, labeled weeks, then repeated the exercise on the oak floor of the living room in carpenter's pencil. *The democracy of math,* he concluded in his notebook: *Can't decide, so I pretend it doesn't matter. But I know it does, or pretend I know, even if not how or why. If there's a mystery, write a formula. Doesn't explain but it reassures.*

After three weeks standing before the easel, adjusting the angle this way and that, moving one of the battered stools from the kitchen into the living room so he could rest his legs, he had used up all but two of his canvases.

Then, one afternoon, he started painting on the wall, about shoulder high, and realized that he'd always wanted to do that.

Developing rules for this game, breaking them as
I go.

1. *Never buy new what can be used.*

2. *House is not home. Don't get comfortable.*

3. *Studio too big a word; call it space.*

4. *Walls and floors can get dirty. Dirty, dirty, dirty. Wish I knew that raising Helen. Could have had more fun, though Edie'd die if she saw. (Already did, dickhead.)*

•   •   •

The first wall painting had no edges, extending out in an awkward, uneven rectangle. It was meant to depict a piece of driftwood Will set alongside three rocks, but even Will admitted the wall revealed little of the original still life he'd constructed on the table. He painted four versions of the same grouping in counterclockwise order—still with no borders, no backgrounds, awkward proportions. By the fourth painting, the driftwood piece had gone squat. No depth, he realized, consulting a how-to book until he learned that a white line along a cylinder on one side near the edge, and some darker paint along the other side edge, can (with some practice, the book warned) give the illusion of reflection and encourage the eye to turn the flat paint round. Or should be able to, he said to himself angrily as his paintings continued to defy the rules.

November 23.

Two days, then Thanksgiving. Driftwood my turkey leg. What next? Frescoes? Murals? Graffiti? No.

5. *But yes to color on the walls.*

6. *Maintain the same still life arrangement until at least two paintings after the first show I'm bored with the setup.*

7. *No new arrangement for two days after any deconstruction.*

8. *Redo each disassembled still life a week or two later to see if it has a life after death.*

9. *Don't worry if you forget what the original looked like. Wrong might be right.*

•   •   •

By early December, Will decided to paint over his wall work.

I don't paint to make a record for others. I'm not an historian anymore. The U.S. needs a national memory dump where we deposit reminders we can't contribute to charities. Or weekly pickups, like garbage, for recycling. Pack the past in plastic bags, stuff it in bins, leave it curbside. There should be a dump reserved for art, toasters, ghosts.

Will bought himself carpenter's white paint at the hardware store and repainted the wall he'd darkened with his five versions of the driftwood and rocks. He took a ruler and divided the wall itself into rectangles as high as he could comfortably reach and as low as he could paint sitting on a pillow. These lines would be his frames. He carried the easel he'd been using into the storage shed, bought a box of ear plugs ("Noise Reduction Rating 31 decibels if worn properly") that he curled into the sides of his head each morning. And began, with the new year, to paint his way across one side of the living room.

2

BY JANUARY, SIX MONTHS AFTER EDIE'S DEATH, Will's life as a painter was as regulated as when he was teaching. *Routine, consistency,* he wrote.

> *Habit is our palette, how we compose days. An offer of perspective, boundary, and the impression of dimension. My habits kept me eating, then caring for Edie. Now they send me walking, beachcombing, painting. We break routine, make new habits. That gives us a split life + awkward transition hours we call consciousness (or shock, or love, or heartbreak) in between. Then what?*

The winter rains and fog blanketed Santa Cruz. Will painted from the time he woke until well after sunset. By ten or eleven at night, he was walking the streets, sometimes until four or five in the morning. He didn't question his new schedule. *Be attentive to, not restrained by, time. Sunrises end my walks, not start my days as they once did.* He remembered, but didn't note, how once Helen left for college, he and Edie would often rise before dawn in the summer and sit quietly together at a spot along the cliffs north of town. They would pause over bread, butter, jam, and a thermos of coffee, maybe walk a beach or read, before heading home to prepare for work.

There were hours when all Will did was rearrange his rock formations on the table, walk around and test angles. He tried to sense what he dismissively called a *right relation of elements.*

> *Failures of structure before failures with paint.*
> *Does a real painter find or build a still life, see*
> *variations as he organizes or after in the paint?*
> *My answer before I picked up a brush was*
> *both/and, but maybe I can take sides on this*
> *before I die? (That word "real"; am I an unreal*
> *painter? Probably.)*

The one decision he came to after a month of painting and repainting his wall was that he needed a more portable surface than the wall itself. He came up with a new plan: ten-by-ten inch pieces of Masonite that he would gesso, paint, then clip on to wires he ran horizontally along the walls. *Walking and waking among boulders,* he wrote one morning. *If I could only get the salt air into the paint.*

●　　　●　　　●

When he wasn't painting, or asleep, Will would walk: one street leading to the next, mile after mile, eventually ending up at a dark beach where he'd sit and watch traces of moonlight reflected in the water. He traveled the same routes for nights at a time until he could predict the domestic patterns: porch lights on at all hours, homes where dogs barked and thrust their jaws at windows or noses through fences, lights in kitchens or dimmer ones in what he guessed must be bathrooms. He could recognize the makes of cars and flatbed trucks alongside homes or in carports. He watched cats who loitered along a window ledge, others who sat on concrete stairways or nestled against a front door. He learned to recognize the occasional whimper or cry, barely audible, that instigated a sequence of lights as (he imagined) parents found their way from bed to child's side. The pale flickering blue TV glow, so alien against the dark, filled what looked like empty rooms. *Family habits my sundial, or darkdial.*

There were more open shades and curtains than Will expected; more people who seemed to enjoy disrobing while staring out at the almost empty streets. But Will found their bodies didn't interest him as much as the play of room light, the way shadows shifted the spatial geometry of an archway into a kitchen, a curved window, ornamental stained glass. He sometimes imagined he was a prehistoric hunter, his eye drawn to movement and sound by shifts of the darkness. He would stop for ten or twenty minutes, stare long enough to distinguish someone eating a snack from someone else writing a note or setting up the coffee maker for the morning. He sometimes checked his watch to see if his route might take him by this or that house at a certain hour where he might find a familiar male or female shape repeating the very same gestures as the day or week before: the bending down that revealed itself as light appearing as the upright body lowered; an arm reaching for something, the frail limb dark against a lit background; someone closing blinds or drawing the curtains.

January 20

> *Nights: still, unknown. Or so I like to think. They*
> *are alive to me as days aren't. No one to see, or*
> *see me. All quiet except me, alley cat, night*
> *prowler. When do I start to howl at the moon?*

One of Will's routes took him along the river, where the homeless congregated under the bridges, their habits shifting only slightly with the weather. By midwinter, he felt he could measure time within a quarter hour, as if families developed migratory instincts like whales or swallows. He began to think of time as a geographic ratio of weights and shadows. And, firmly as he held to a belief in his own impetuosity choosing one route over another, he had to concede that he was as essential to the system as the newspaper delivery cars that captivated him between five and six each morning.

Why this new carnal love of matter in me? he asked himself in the notebook entry for February 4.

> *Stones, streets, concrete, tar, bridges, lamps,*
> *moon, porch lights, water, metal fences, walls:*
> *my chemistry. The smell of air preparing for*
> *rain, the day's leftovers, gravel, the sidewalk in*
> *fog. Beaker of solitude.*

It was mid-February before Will realized with surprise that he'd passed through Martin Luther King's birthday and the end of the school semester in January without a blink. "Lesson plan life," was Edie's phrase for the way Will sometimes neglected everything but his classes once a school year began.

"When's the unit on 'wife and child,' Mr. History?" she'd ask.

It was not just conscientiousness that forced Will's attention away from himself and his family. He never learned to plan, so always felt behind. He fumbled his way along, never sure what he was going to do until he did it. Edie was the opposite, her work schedule as tidy as her kitchen counters. She taught her classes, corrected the student homework before she got home, kept files of her handouts. Compact, complete, successful. She tried to help Will see the value of organization: "If you don't worry about what's ahead, you can see where you are" was her refrain. She tried once—just once—to assemble Will's notes into an ordered sequence, but her structure disappeared into his waywardness in less than a month.

•   •   •

In late winter, Will rearranged his walks to coincide with the town's weekly cycle of garbage pickups. By midnight, the cans would line the curb: brown for garbage; blue for recycling; green for grass, weeds, and branches. Will would open one garbage can after another, block after block. He would mostly just glance, occasionally stick his hand inside to feel around the plastic bags or into the piles of papers, pulling things up to stare at with a tiny flashlight.

He got to know people by their trash, from the cans that were rinsed each week and prepared for the next load of neatly packed white, black, or clear plastic bags to the more helter-skelter families, with their mixes of plastic and paper, random diapers and batteries, pizza boxes and limp lettuce—the refuse as disordered as, he imagined, their days. He rarely kept anything—a child's drawing, a letter or stamp, a broken handle from a toy, a bit of clothes worn to some color he prized, a cracked mug, bottle, or broken dish. Most of his keepsakes found their way into his own garbage soon after, though he would sometimes spend an hour struggling to reproduce the color of a blouse or skirt, or keep this or that mug or bowl around for a week. He never went out to the town dump, where he might have climbed mountains of waste—

> *Too big, too anonymous, too daytime, too*
> *obvious. I want my crap in pieces, labeled—*
> *family, house, neighborhood, night. What's been*
> *given up on when, without knowing who or why.*
> *Don't want to imagine I'm recycling in a useful*
> *way. (Does that make art useless?)*

Will consciously avoided words like "happy" or "sad" in his mind and his notebook. "Denial has its merits," he remembered Edie repeating when he'd rant about the government's blind eye to poverty, racial profiling, or another of the hypocrisies that kept him in despair about America. What he knew was that he had found a way to pass his days. He felt comfortable honing to the patterns he'd created. He resisted asking himself why he'd created this way to live and not another; why isolation, silence, and darkness felt so safe. If he wasn't quite content, he was not discontented, and that seemed to him enough. For now, he sometimes added to himself.

•   •   •

What Will was not prepared for that quiet stormy winter was Kitty.

All his life she took him by surprise, this woman he loved and barely knew. He was on his fourth row of Masonite squares the day she rang the bell. Will ignored the sound until it was joined by a muffled banging that seemed to come from knee level. He peeked through a side window and saw Kitty standing there, her hand raised to ring again, her face turned downward to a boy standing by her side. The boy clutched one of her fingers in his stubby fist while he used his other to bang doggedly at the wooden door.

Kitty had been in Will's life almost as long as Edie. "Ms. Fairweather," he called her—though not often, since the nickname annoyed Edie. For years he dismissed Kitty as a seasonal blip on the weather charts, a Holly Golightly who drifted in and out of town avoiding the rains and chill. What was she doing here now, he wondered?

He stood, staring through the peephole at Kitty and the boy. He hesitated, afraid. He knew he had to open the door, though not sure why, or what would happen when he did.

"Love me, love her," Edie warned Will the first time they had Kitty and her husband, Howard, over for dinner. Will found her flighty, self-focused. He never could pinpoint what he was reacting to, but the feeling persisted for years—that resistance to Kitty for being so completely who she was.

"You keep looking for happiness like you're prospecting for gold, Kitty," he remembered telling her, determined to get beneath her hardy, nearly insufferable, nonchalance. "Like it's 1848, and you're heading for California to beat the rush that hasn't happened yet."

"I'm just more curious than you are, Will," she answered, barely turning her eyes up from the magazine she was forever glancing through, her attention always split between people and the glossy pictures. "You've got Edie to keep you happy; I have my whims."

They took her, those whims, everywhere the sails of fad and impulse could carry her. When did it start, he asked himself that afternoon after she and Benny left? Was it twenty years ago? More?

At least twenty, he decided. A Saturday, late summer. She had just returned from what, until then, was her annual two weeks with Howard's family in Kentucky to inform Edie that she was getting a divorce.

"It was the day we went to see Gettysburg," she said, turning her face to Will to let him make an historical nod, though he had never actually been to the battlefield in all his years of Civil War reading.

"I looked up and there it was. A blue sky, a great white puff of cloud, and an eagle. Huge, the kind they'd hire for a movie. You have to picture it. Total quiet, and this bird soaring on the currents. Gliding. Then just one or two almost slow-motion flaps of its wings. We're on our way to Gettysburg accompanied by an eagle, like in some song. I made Howard pull over. When he finally got to some turnoff he thought was wide enough—miles and minutes later—I rushed Sam out of the back seat so she could see. I'm pointing this marvel out to our daughter when Howard pipes up, 'It's a vulture, not an eagle.'"

She stopped, expecting a reaction, Will remembered. She must have seen something in Edie's eyes because she jumped on:

"Exactly. I stood there, Sam in my arms, staring at Howard across the top of the Chevy we'd rented looking up at his stupid vulture. When I got back in the car, I knew I didn't want to spend the rest of my life with someone who looked at eagles and saw vultures. I told him I was leaving that night," she added with a finality underlined by her radiant smile.

"It was like I gave myself wings, Edie," she said, pushing the metaphor too far as she pushed everything and everyone too far—or so Will felt. He liked Howard, a cardiologist who spent his off-hours making old clocks and watches tick again. Chances are what they saw was a vulture, Will knew, not an eagle. But Kitty was taking off anyway, whatever winged creature was responsible for her flight.

She left the ground with an excitement that turned every detail into a high-wire act. Her life, and stories, depended on the word "very" (*as mine did the word "maybe,"* he admitted to himself that night in his notebook).

Kitty insisted on very rich red lipstick, showed Edie the very high heels on the new shoes she'd just bought in this very posh store in San Francisco next to the perfect hair salon where they weren't afraid to cut your hair very

very short. HRE—Her Royal Extremis—he'd sometimes mouth to Edie as he handed her the phone to take a call from Kitty, whom Edie adored with a love as indifferent to Kitty's incautiousness as to lint on her sweaters. "Messages from the poles" was how Edie liked to describe Kitty's postcards. Helen, just a teen then, pasted the cards across one wall of her bedroom and lined her dresser drawers with a patchwork of the stamps.

"Kitty's my Captain Kirk, Will," Edie often insisted. "You need to look up at the stars more often yourself. Do you good."

"Arles in October is what lets Hollywood imagine technicolor," Kitty wrote in one of her breathless notes that first fall, when she stayed a month in Southern France before moving on to Italy ("too many statues, lovely bodies, marvelous cheese"), then Crete for the winter before sweeping back to the U. S. through Sicily, a three-week invitation offered by the heir of some olive groves she met on a beach. ("Young pup of a boy, lapdog charm, acreage, chest hair, sex. Wine needs aging, but very abundant.") And there were the Prague years, three or four, he couldn't quite remember, when she swore that she was through with the U.S., and was remodeling hotel lobbies in Stockholm, Paris, Lausanne, Barcelona, Glasgow. ("The Scotch aren't penny-pinching like the stories say. Sweetest louts with a few stouts in them. But dull. Calluses seem to have migrated from their hands to their brains.")

She made regular trips to Norway, where family connections helped her import a line of handsome oil lamps that found their way into exclusive stores and elegant catalogues. And to Thailand, where she apprenticed herself to a puppet master, and returned with hundreds of beautiful shadow puppets which she sold, slowly, a few at a time, to collectors who trusted her taste and tiny museums in obscure Midwestern towns anxious to fill out their multicultural room. And shorter stints: two journeys to India wandering from ashram to ashram; time in a Japanese monastery. Will remembered an apprenticeship with Native American shamans in New Mexico and Arizona; even weeks hammering nails with Habitat for Humanity in Ghana. ("All these years imagining interiors and only now do I spend my nights pulling out splinters.")

Kitty kept a house in Santa Cruz—the one Howard gave her in the divorce. That was home, she liked to say, where she knew she was welcome so didn't have to stay. She'd appear one day at their front door with more energy, excitement, and presents than they knew what to do with, ready to spend two or three months in town refurnishing a room, visiting her acupuncturist, or traveling to San Francisco to find wall hangings. Will and Edie were her oldest friends, she always said—her first stop, and last. She'd grown up with Edie—which really meant they'd met in college and shared an apartment for three years before Howard, and eventually Edie's first husband, Frank, entered their lives and friendship. The gift Kitty had for knowing what other people like her wanted, along with the money Howard provided in the divorce settlement and later in his will, gave her the freedom to follow her whims wherever they led.

Kitty was in Edie's and Will's lives as often in absence as in body—which was more or less fine with Will. Will got used to Kitty's reports from alien galaxies. He never confessed to Edie that he came to miss the high tension of Kitty's vocabulary of pleasure and crisis as she gradually muted in language, color scheme, and tremolo in the decades following her divorce, while she spread herself like a soft sheet over the world. He kept his decreasing skepticism and advancing affection veiled under polite nods and begrudging shrugs in response to Edie's constant delight in her friend.

Kitty truncated her movements the year before Edie died, hopping between Santa Cruz and Juneau, where she bought, remodeled, and sold three houses. When she was in town, Kitty's bedside stays were filled with reports on Alaskan labor, her struggles to get the right materials at the right time, and the final, astronomical-to-Will sales prices— these her contributions to cheer up the dogged Edie between her chemo sessions. When Edie turned really, irretrievably, sick, Kitty stopped traveling to be with her "lodestar," as she liked to call Edie—to her face and, more often, to Will, nights when the two of them sat at the dining room table over a glass of wine or tea while Edie slept. She left before the end—about a month before—and wasn't there for the funeral: "I can cry without company," she wrote Will on a postcard showing a bear standing in ankle-deep snow before a series of white-capped mountains. He hadn't seen her since, though every week there was another postcard from somewhere else he'd never been: China, Yugoslavia, South Africa, Boston—if he remembered the last address right.

•   •   •

"William. I know you are in there. It's rainy. I'm cold. Let us in."

He did, pulling open the door with what he hoped passed as excited surprise.

"What, my dear, has happened to you?" was the first thing Kitty said. "I've tried calling for days to no avail; have you given up on your answering machine?"—all this tumbling from her while she pushed herself and the little boy past him with a soft kiss on one of his paint-smeared cheeks.

"This is Benny, Will," she said, barely glancing at her host. "Benny, shake hands please."

The boy looked up at Will and reached out a soft hand, which Will took in his and held for a moment. Will saw a round, soft, shy face and brown eyes. A beanie covered the boy's head and his small body was lost in a bright yellow raincoat. Kitty quickly unclasped the coat and pulled off the hat, revealing a pale buzz of hair dotted with a few drops of rain. The boy moved quickly towards the living room.

Kitty turned back to Will and, with a laugh, exclaimed, "You look awful. When's the last time you shaved?"

It was Kitty's laugh that echoed still later that night. That, and the realization that he'd likely not shaved for months—or even looked in a mirror. He was dressed as he always dressed: in his paint-spattered jeans and once-white shirt, the frayed tails hanging over his belt and belly, the sleeves rolled up just above his elbows, his feet bare. He held a paintbrush in one hand. When he taught, he had prided himself on his appearance, carefully ironing—and even starching—the button-down shirts he wore to school each morning.

While Will watched, immobilized in the hallway, Kitty's bemused smile and tender eyes turned back and forth between him and the boy, as if at a ping-pong match. Flushed and angry, unsure what to do with himself, Will stared at and then past her out to the rain hitting the porch. He didn't move. It was Kitty who closed the door, a signal to Will to welcome her with a cautious hug.

Kitty looked the same as when she left, he thought: the same raven-black hair cut short and spiked; the same dark crimson lipstick; the same (or new, he presumed, but similarly styled) dark leather jacket beneath the slicker she threw off and handed to Will, who had no idea where to put it. Bright red checks across her Western shirt and new dark blue jeans had replaced the long black skirt and elegant blouses she was wearing the last time he had seen her in June. He was angry at her then for deserting him through Edie's last weeks. But grateful, it turned out, not to see her through the summer. The postcards she sent while she circled the globe were intrusions enough.

Kitty turned from Will toward the living room and stopped, arrested by the sight. Benny, unaccustomed to anything else, had already darted forward, heading for a hill of rocks that occupied the far corner of the room.

"Redecorating without me?" she asked as she turned back to Will, glued in his tracks.

Standing behind her, Will looked at the room through her eyes: the rocks, the barren oak floor with its pencil arcs encircling the dining room table, a tarp over the windows, the bland grays, blacks, and browns of rock and driftwood.

Her comment was somehow comforting—unexpected and exactly right—as Kitty so often was when she could assume that speculative, slightly distant stance she took when confronted by sincerity. She would, Will knew, remember very different furnishings—worn, inelegant, comfortable. "Growing-up decor," Edie liked to call it when Kitty would tease her and offer some ideas about alternative couches, rugs, or wall colors.

What Will offered Kitty now was a mound of rocks where Benny was struggling with great effort to get a foothold so he could ascend, his rain boots making the smallest slipping noise, like rubbed sand. The rocks sat there, formal as the stacked cannon balls one sometimes saw at old forts or war monuments, but twice as tall, at least up to Kitty's chest. The stack was surrounded by a scatter of other rocks and pieces of driftwood, so it seemed like a quarter of the room had been given over to some construction site. Across the room was a smaller pile of broken bottles and utensils that looked like remnants from a rowdy party. There were thin brown tinted bottles without caps and smaller square ones that looked like they once held some upscale vinegar. A stocky cobalt blue container, no doubt from an inkstand, was creased on one side by a thin crack. That sat alongside a stout bright yellow pitcher without a handle. A silver-plated wine cup leaned precariously on the pitcher, one side slightly flattened where it seemed to have been banged by a hammer. There were boxes with lids and without, some round, some square, one rectangular.

The dining room table sat before the cold, closed fireplace. The white sheet that covered it was smudged with a random spray of pale browns, tans, and soft blues, an occasional spot of red or yellow, and small flecks of black. Near the edge sat four large dark rocks, three nearly flat and not quite touching each other; the fourth more angular, leaning on one of the others.

Then there were the walls, divided now into rectangles by thick vertical and horizontal black lines of paint. At various times, Will would decide the lines made the wall look like it was a room-size version of the periodic table or a vast tic-tac-toe game waiting for the Xs and Os. The spaces waist-high and above were filled with his Masonite squares, each covered with paint, hanging at a slight forward pitch off the wires Will had strung along his checkerboard-painted grid.

If Kitty had asked, Will could have explained how the groupings in each painting varied: sometimes one or two rocks, sometimes three or four (never more); sometimes with the rocks flat, sometimes standing; sometimes all leaning on each other; sometimes one or two in front and the others behind; sometimes one absent; sometimes filling the painted space and other times smaller, with a horizon line to indicate table's edge. He might have explained that some were one-offs, others designed as a series featuring the same or nearly the same rock group rearranged. Two paintings that stood out for him hung near the bottom of the wall—rocks alongside broken bottles and other glassware, the cracks painted bright red in one piece, a shining black in the other.

Kitty didn't say a word. She walked over to the wall and let her hand graze the surface of the Masonite squares. As she stared, Will watched the smile turn down on her face despite what he imagined were her efforts to the contrary.

These were ugly, awkward messes, he knew—globs of paint pretending to form; unbalanced compositions; skewed perspectives. They lacked shading and reflection—not to mention a sense of bulk in space—and Will knew Kitty's aesthetic muscles must be twitching despite herself.

"My Goldberg Variations," Will said as she turned to him.

"I'm not sure Bach would recognize them," was Kitty's reply.

Will tried to see what he thought she saw—the transformation or undoing of a lifetime—without giving up what he himself was trying to see—how to paint rocks. Or paint anything at all. How to give over to a passion. How to occupy his empty hours. He looked at his wall, with its collection of inept paintings, and back through the days and months it had taken to paint them. He was aware of the disconnect between the art and the hours he spent on each canvas—hours when he was absorbed, attentive to rock and paint, eager to discover what rocks might reveal given the chance to interact before his eyes and under his brush.

Will's notes—some complete sentences, others near incoherent jottings—recorded what he thought he was trying to do, or trying to find out how to do. *To lean on something, rock against rock: is one thing supporting another, or only holding it in place? What—or who, when it's humans—depends on who? What support does the supported offer the supporter?* he wrote early in January.

A few days later, his attention shifted to issues of space:

If two things are proximate, with room between them, is that space they create negative space like art books call it or positive—like, say, two lovers

*sitting on a park bench. How much or little space
between encourages us to view the two things
together versus separately? What happens when
a third object is added? Can the third piece just
be alone, or is it inevitably lonely? Views of
marriage seem to insist on attention.*

That curiosity led him to another:

*Where is depth in the surface? Books say you
create the illusion of it with placement, size,
intensity: before and behind, larger and smaller,
darker and lighter. That doesn't quite compute, or
not yet. Either the theories are wrong, or my brain
invents more worlds than an eye can compass.*

Two days before Kitty appeared, his attention had
shifted yet again, to edges and broken lines:

*No borders in nature, my art book says. Does it
help to know this, or imagine this as true? Can a
black edge alter my perspective on a rock? Its
neighbor? And what lives inside the darkness of
the border line itself?*

*Why is a crack worth noticing? The lightning
analogy—a shock from God or clouds, interceding
in the stone with a message, however
indecipherable. What remains of it after repair,
in that faint line that never quite disappears?
What's cracking up, what's taking new form? Like
light leakage into the past? Like tomato sauce
stains from the pasta you never quite remove from
the plate, your pants, your memory?*

•   •   •

It was Benny who helped Will and Kitty through the next hour. They heard a startled cry followed by several loud thuds. They turned to see a small avalanche of boulders as Benny slid down the rock hill onto his back. He started to pull himself up, but a rock dropped onto his hand. He screamed and waved his right hand in the air, thumb and index finger bright red and ready to swell.

Kitty reached him first, lifting him in her arms. Will turned in the opposite direction, to the kitchen for ice cubes and a towel. He handed them to Kitty, then headed along the back hallway into the bathroom searching for bandages. He hoped he hadn't cleaned those out with the hair dryer.

When he returned with what he could find—a flattened cardboard box holding a few tired Band-Aids with figures of animals on their surface—Kitty was sitting on the floor, Benny howling in her lap. She tried to rock him and keep the ice pack against his finger while she looked up at Will with a face that seemed more ready to laugh than collapse in worry. He watched her from a distance, their eyes meeting over the boy's head a couple times while he lifted the scattered stones back into place. Will's movements gradually got the boy's attention; his wails quieted to sniffles.

Will had seldom seen Kitty in this motherly role, but she took to it with the same grace, he realized, as when she gardened or played hostess at one of her lavish dinners—one broad hand cupped around Benny's head, the other pushing the ice onto his hand. She chattered to the boy—words Will couldn't quite make out, but was sure were meant for comfort: a Kitty coo. By the time Will moved towards the two of them with his bandages, the bruised fingers—thumb and index, it turned out—were already turning an exquisite mixture of yellow, blue, and purple. (What I'd give if I could mix colors like that, Will caught himself thinking.) The bandages, adorned with pictures of pelicans and sea lions, completed the first aid.

"Ever seen anything like these?" Will asked the sniffling child as he slowly let himself down on the ground.

He pulled the soiled protective plastic from one side of the bandages after the other and gently patted them onto Benny's two fingers, adding an unnecessary third and fourth bandage over the others to make sure Benny appreciated the extent of his wound.

"Once there were these pelicans, Ace and Cross, who lived on the edge of the pier here in town. Ever been to the pier?"

A slow back-and-forth "No" of the head.

"If you look down through the boards, you'll see these huge sea lions lying on the wooden beams like they were couches. They lie there all day, not doing anything but calling to each other. Sea lions have horrible voices, like sick dogs. You know what a sick dog sounds like? No? Come on, let me hear what you think a sick dog sounds like."

And while the boy tried to belch out a whimper of pain that he imagined might come from an ailing pup, Will himself let out a moan like a bleating warehouse horn announcing the end of the workday. He startled Kitty, who was still wiping the tears from Benny's cheeks, and made her turn her face up to his. The story, he realized, was as old as the bandage box itself—bought to patch some bruise of Helen's with adhesive and distract her with adventure. He didn't realize how much of the tale he remembered.

"You know what a pelican is, right? Good. You should go out to the pier with your grandmother and watch them sometimes, whipping along."

Will glanced up at Kitty, who was looking at him while her hand kept softly rubbing the hair from Benny's forehead.

"Not eagles, but pretty," he said, more to her than the boy.

Then he looked down at Benny again.

"So Ace and Cross lived at the edge of the pier and would swoop along just over the water like they were on skis. Every so often they'd dive into the water for a fish and fly off with it in their mouth pouch. They were pretty cool birds because, even though they flew away in the winter, they always came back and sat on these same two pilings at the very end of the pier, where they could watch everything. Sat there, right above the sea lions. The pelicans didn't especially like the sea lions—you can understand what it must be like to listen to that sound all day, right?"

Will waited for a nod.

"And the sea lions did their best to ignore the birds—pesky creatures that would dive and leap around. And poop on them. Not on purpose, but you know how birds poop, all that white gloppy stuff, right down onto the snoring lions."

Will lifted his hand and let it drift down onto Benny's arm like something released from the clouds, while the boy shrugged the hand off, but kept his stare on Will's face.

Will went on with his tale, to a night when Ace and Cross helped the sea lions during a blinding winter storm, how the birds started dropping little bits of fish for the large creatures to catch, how the pelicans learned to dine on the leftovers of sea lion feasts. He played the story for laughs, the way he remembered doing decades ago for Helen with variations to fit the occasion, year after year, until the bandages disappeared into that drawer where he had just found them—disappeared along with Helen's faith that he had the power to heal whatever bruise life had in store.

Benny was sitting up by this time. He pushed his way out of Kitty's lap. Will went on a moment longer, to the fun the birds had pooping on local teens who would drunkenly come to harass the lions. Benny struggled to his feet, his gaze wandering across the living room.

Sensing the boy's inattention, Will stopped himself in mid-sentence, lifted Benny to the top of the rock pile, and held his hand while the boy balanced himself. Benny swayed slightly from side to side, then slowly pulled his hand away to test his stance. Just as Will stood back, Benny pushed himself into the air in a little leap, plopped down with a yell onto his butt, and slid down the bumpy edge of the rocks. He finished with a laugh of triumph as he hit the floor and quickly bounced up and off, traveling two loops around the startled, laughing adults before disappearing down the hallway, leaving Will and Kitty breathless in his wake.

Will turned a newly embarrassed smile to his guest and, holding her elbow with the edges of his paint-stained fingers, pulled Kitty upright and kissed her on one cheek, then the other. She reached a tentative hand to his face and rubbed it along Will's beard for an instant. Then he turned her towards the dining room and kitchen at the back of the house—rooms still more or less as he knew she knew them except for the absent dining room table. He could offer her tea, and did, though with the caution that he had nowhere for her to sit save the two stools that stood by the counter. But there were three small boxes of tea bags: Earl Grey, Herbal, Green Leaf. Beside them sat a jar of honey in a bowl of water. "The ants invading again?" Kitty asked, while Will pulled up the thick honey from the sides of the jar with a spoon. He nodded.

•　　　•　　　•

Kitty and Benny were the first people to walk through Will's front door since Helen left. For the rest of the afternoon, he heard their voices echo through every corner of his once-silent house. He was annoyed with Kitty for wanting to see him, annoyed at himself for letting her, annoyed even more that now, alone, hours later, walking the familiar, quiet streets, he couldn't stop thinking about her or himself through her gaze. He saw Will the teacher and husband Kitty first knew, his life given over to Edie and Helen, his students, and reading; then Will over the last two years as Edie's caretaker, conscientious and selfless. Now she returned from her travels to meet Will the recluse, his days measured in paint and rocks, food and his journal, walks and garbage cans.

Will and Kitty were lovers when she left. Their hours together felt inevitable after the hand squeezes and hugs of consolation they shared in waiting rooms, at the front door morning and night, in the kitchen as they moved from counter to refrigerator preparing Edie's meals or boiling water for her tea. Will sometimes offered Kitty a brief back and shoulder massage when she stood at the sink washing dishes. She'd relax against him with a quiet "hmmm" of contentment, her hands deep in suds or circling a sponge over a plate or bowl.

The first kiss surprised him as he leaned across the car to offer her his accustomed lips on the cheek after driving her home. He didn't know if she just turned at the wrong moment, or by design. Or if he in fact moved her face closer with a finger on her cheek. He didn't know, either, whether he was responding to her announcement the day before that she was leaving soon, or just to her being there, night after night, day after day. And he never asked.

Kitty pulled back from his lips, but not until her own had opened under his for an instant. She looked into his eyes then, shrouded in the shadow of the car, before her hand went to the back of his head to pull him forward—at least as he remembered the moment. From there, through the next hour or a little more, and the few days before she left, he felt released, reassured of something he already knew about her affection for him, and his for her, that he hadn't acknowledged.

They undressed each other slowly that first night, moving into Kitty's bedroom holding hands, quiet after the one exchange of "Are you sure this is OK with you?" from her; his soundless, uncertain lift of shoulders followed by a nod and return question, "And with you?" and her soundless hand squeeze in answer.

They discovered they knew a lot about each other's bodies with so little touch over so many years, and played with a passion and demand that surprised him. He always imagined her breasts smaller than they were, though he had watched with admiration as her hips and rear, trim and tight from yoga, spread and widened along with thigh and waist. He was a little surprised by the flip of belly he found, like a flap of skin or overhang of small flowers on a balcony ledge, that rested below her belly button. She opened to him easily, touched him and took him into her mouth and body with relish, laughed at his hunger and the way he hissed through clenched teeth as he came.

Their talk as they lay in bed next to each other was about Edie. No autopsies, postmortems, inspections of anatomy. Or none after that first night, when his hands roved over Kitty lying alongside with a wonder he didn't know he had in him. He remembered that feeling—at once entirely contented and avid, eager. She let his hand move where it wanted while she stared quietly at her ceiling, her own hand resting on his thigh. Then, with a laugh, she took his hand and put it between her legs, reached for his penis, turned sideways as he grew erect and then sat atop him, offering her breasts to his mouth. It was years since he'd come twice in an evening; years when he'd resigned himself to his diminished desires, needs, and capacities; years when he contented himself with Edie's affectionate nighttime kiss, her hand holding his, the way her thigh dropped across his leg when she fell into sleep.

Still he was convinced, and thought she believed too, that it was Edie whom they found so comforting, even adored, in each other. She warned him that first night: "Will, this is lovely, you are lovely. I care so much about you. But I am leaving. I can't watch Edie die. I can't and won't. So don't count on me."

Will nodded, answered back that he'd be fine. He had enough on his mind imagining life without Edie not to add self-pity about Kitty's disappearance—so predictable, so consistent with so much else in her life. He missed her body sometimes those first days after she left. Memories of her would suddenly lodge in his thoughts as he drove around town or sat alone at his night vigils. But he'd long been a distracted partner to Edie, so his wandering mind could hardly have surprised her. He was never sure if she knew about Kitty and him. He hoped that if she did imagine something, she was fine with it, knowing Kitty was Kitty and her friend for life, and Will was always there for her, always hers.

And he was. The nights with Kitty were wonderful—an extraordinary, immense pleasure. There was an intensity to her that startled him—a hard, demanding movement over and under him, a firm pull on his hand adjusting fingers or palm, a soft give of flesh in the underside of her arm below the armpit that he loved to suck on as much as he did her tits. Even in his and Edie's most ardent years of sex, their laughter was as frequent as their moments lost in passion. Sex with Kitty was something else: not friendly, not comic. Demanding, her need calling out needs of his own he didn't know he had. After Edie died, he thought about Kitty often, but randomly, particularly when her postcards arrived. But she didn't call, or he didn't answer if she did. He didn't try to track her down. He didn't even ask himself why he hadn't tried to contact her until now—the night after she pushed her way through the door he thought he'd firmly closed on his past.

As he stalked the silent streets that night, Will tried to imagine what it must have been like for Kitty, walking through that door—as known to her as any in the world—

to find herself in a foreign landscape. Kitty's my walking obituary if I have one, Will thought, like it or not—the one person besides Helen who knows me longest, even best. And knows me as Helen never can: as husband, as lover. Maybe not as friend, Will thought to himself, but Will had never really had many of those. Except for Edie, he corrected himself. Always except for Edie.

Will knew Kitty well enough to know that answering or not answering the door would do no good with her—especially while she had a companion like Benny curious to explore a house as full of wonders as his. He walked for hours that night, uncomfortable in ways he had not been just twenty-four hours before, with the darkness and the steady, penetrating rain that soaked his jeans and shoes. He flayed the air with his arms as if warding off an attack.

When he got home, he felt uncomfortable in his house. He climbed up his ladder and sat on the roof, staring off into the darkness, letting the rain soak through his pants and jacket and drip slowly down his face. He looked with bleak resignation at the invasions to come, as sure of his inability to prevent them as he had been the year before of his inability to save Edie. Helen he could avoid—at least for a time. The friendships of his teaching life had easily eroded before his indifference. But Kitty seemed still to require the sky around her to be filled with eagles. And what were a few rocks to that kind of wingspread?

3

THOUGH HE CONTINUED TO MUMBLE TO HIMSELF that Kitty and Benny were a nuisance, Will opened his door to them whenever they knocked. He plugged in his phone, went with them to the pier, bought Benny fish heads and tails, and showed him how to drop them down to the sea lions and offer them to the greedy pelicans and gulls. If the sun was out, he and Kitty would occupy a picnic table while Benny talked to the fishermen who lined the end of the pier, returning with tales of crabs, rockfish, and ling cod. Will created new adventures for Ace and Cross, pointing up the coast to buoys where the birds liked to play and insisting Kitty produce sketches of the sea lions lying across the intricate crossbeams.

For her part, Kitty accommodated herself to Will's sleeping habits. There were late afternoons when Kitty would sit at Will's house for two or three hours with her magazines, playing grandmother and art advisor in turn. Will was surprised that he wasn't self-conscious in front of her; he found he could paint as if she weren't there. She didn't seem to mind the silence, glancing up only rarely (if his own infrequent, surreptitious side views her way were an accurate gauge) to look at his work.

The closest he and Kitty came to admitting their alliance was a week after Kitty's reentry into Will's life. He asked her, almost casually, how long she planned to be around. She looked up at him and smiled.

"Long enough to annoy you, and get this boy feeling loved again. Maybe show you something about depth and volume."

"Or until you get antsy."

"Or you do, Rembrandt," she answered.

Will had heard little about Benny over the years. Was he four? five? Will never doubted Kitty's affection. But Kitty was Kitty. She never appeared grandmotherly in that way Edie took to like chocolate—addictively, Will felt at times, her days and nights filled with long phone calls to Helen discussing eating habits, TV rules, bedtimes. He imagined Kitty's presence in the boy's life as like her presence in his own: unconditional, intense, impulsive, and intermittent.

One day when the boy was taking a nap on the mattress in Helen's room, he asked Kitty why Benny was with her.

"My own damn fault, I suppose," she said. "Samantha's inherited my wanderlust."

Kitty laughed. "At least my lust."

Will felt himself blush, but kept dabbing his brush at the Masonite as if he hadn't registered Kitty's joke.

"Turn around, Will," she said. "I'm tired of talking to your back."

He did. She sighed.

"Samantha's left Evan. She got involved with someone at Santa Barbara where she teaches. A visiting hotshot in physics. She's gone back home with him, to Boston. Evan's a wreck."

"And you've come to the rescue."

"Temporarily. Until they figure out what's next."

"Does Benny know what's going on?"

"He's a little confused about cause and effect. 'Daddy's sick, so Mommy went away with Mr. Torchi until he gets better,' is what he said to the gardener yesterday."

"He told me that you're taking him for a vacation," Will said to Kitty.

"That's my story and I'm sticking to it," she said, looking at him with a smile before she bent her head down to the magazine in her lap.

Will nodded and turned back to his painting.

•   •   •

Will's house offered Benny a world of invention. Will retrieved a box of toys and books Edie had kept in the shed for the grandchildren. They were a start: enough Legos and wood blocks to build blockades; stacks of paper and colored markers; a toddler plastic caboose that Benny used to whiz down the hall and bang into walls. Kitty provided other props: a flag on a long stick; two squirt gun rifles, a rubber tomahawk, and several plastic grenades that Benny hid in rock crevices around the living room. Will let these pass, though he'd never allowed his grandchildren to bring weapons into the house.

Then there were the temperas that Kitty bought Benny so he could stand behind or beside Will, at the child easel Will pulled back into the living room. Will tore up some cardboard boxes to create painting surfaces, and the boy would paint blue and red versions of the still lifes Will constructed. Will pinned the paintings along a wall in the hall, as orderly and neighborly one with another as his own meek efforts. *My eyes feel old, fogged,* he wrote to himself in the middle of March.

> *Benny's are young, unashamed (or is this adult sentimentality?). I'm abashed by Benny's studies: no depth, but no disappointment in its absence. Primary colors without worry about shading. So much for attention, study, books. Or maybe this is what attention is?*

·   ·   ·

Will's painting was going through what he derisively referred to as his "analytic" stage. Will had long ago convinced himself that what he needed to know or wanted to find out could be learned from a book. And (a legacy from the '60s) to distrust everything he read. From then on, he embraced both of his faiths—that books were the solution and the problem—as truths without worrying that they were contradictory, or what that contradiction might mean. Now he was skeptical of both ideas, which left him in more or less the same position. But since he didn't want to talk to anyone, but did want to try to figure out how to paint, he bought himself what primers he could—used when he could find them, to stay true to his scavenging policy.

The directions he found were both repetitious and self-canceling, all of them requiring some basis of arm-hand control he'd never possessed. He realized too what he'd long felt as a teacher: that you could only really teach people what they already knew. And when it came to looking at the world, he realized he knew very little—or little that was useful. The books explained that what he did remember— the shape or shades of a rock, a face, a bottle, or a crack— was a hindrance. What was required instead was unwashed, uncooked seeing: the perspective dictated by the thing rather than the preconception: *Precedent gives art rules, but keeps the viewer from seeing. True of law as well?* Will asked himself.

Most of what the books offered Will thought of as a series of hand tricks: how to use light and dark and thin and thick lines to indicate shadow or foregrounding, how opposites on the color wheel worked on the eye.

I've listened to too many people for too long, Will wrote one Thursday in late March, a day spent alone after begging off Kitty's insistent entreaties to drive to San Francisco.

Read too many books giving me too many prescriptions. The pills pile up, the gout is never cured. The recipes grind down the mind, like waves do the rocks. Old age is mostly erosion, rough air. With rocks residue gets worn away, with people residue shows in sagging skin, lined faces, varicose veins. Is that what my paintings lack—the shadows under my eyes?

Will's brain was awash with suggestions about atmospheric and one-point, two-point, and three-point perspective; light and tone; negative space; ground and figure; brush strokes and shadow; color relations and boundary. He nailed a small checklist to the mantel, elements of art he decided he needed to keep in mind:

> *color*
> *shape*
> *mass*
> *light*
> *space*
> *shadow*
> *setting*
> *scale*

He kept them in mind, but ticking them off did no good, since he had no idea what each of these elements were, let alone what they might have to do with each other. *Are objects contingent? relative? relatives?* Will asked himself in his notebook.

> *Or only contingent in the stories we tell about what paintings represent? Or is it—are we—all contingent, leaning on others to stay upright, always dependent, and unregenerate on our own? Contingent to what, or which whats (or whos)?*

And, the next day:

> *Do these concepts—of light, space, scale—control the material, the canvas, the artist? Does a rock*

apprehend shadow? proximity? Does it matter if it doesn't?

To escape his list, Will decided to concentrate on just one thing at a time. He abandoned his palette for shades of gray so he could learn at least a little something about light before he tried to figure out bulk, let alone color.

●　　　●　　　●

In the midst of these early spring afternoons with Kitty, as the rains came in random alternation with a cold sun, Will started to talk again. Benny might be outside, where Will gave him free rein to wander through the boxes in the storage shed, or standing at his child easel, painting with energetic abandon. Kitty would be sitting as she usually did, on a canvas director's chair she'd brought over to Will's house once she realized he had nothing but pillows and his two kitchen stools to sit on. At first, all Will offered were curt, cautious answers to Kitty's infrequent and random—or seemingly random—questions while he walked here and there in the living room staring at his rocks, the paint brush in his hand, or tried a few strokes on the Masonite boards. But gradually his talks with Kitty, or his reconstructions of them when she left and he was alone, became a way to talk to himself.

●　　　●　　　●

"The rocks," Kitty began one day, head lowered to the magazine in front of her.

"Hmmm?"

"You steal them?"

"Yes and no. Take them. From the beaches, and sometimes people's front yards. You know how old folks will give up the lawn thing and fill their yards with boulders or make borders around a square of dirt with stones."

"You steal them. And you're one of the old folks."

"I suppose. Yes."

"On your walks. When no one's looking."

"On my walks."

"Where do you go, remind me?"

"It varies. One area for a few days, until I know the streets. Then another. Been by your house more than a few times. Always dark."

Kitty let that pass.

"Towards the water."

"And away."

"To sit."

"Sit, look at people, watch the waves if the moon's out."

"Why?"

"It's dark and quiet. I can see then."

"And can't be seen?"

"Right. I try to make sure of that."

"What do you see? Besides what you steal, I mean."

"Houses, rooms, yards, cars. I don't steal much. Unless looking is stealing. I'm not hurting anyone."

"It sounds to me like you've decided nights are exotic, romantic, exceptional."

"Not exceptional. Darkness makes me curious; days don't. That's all I know. Maybe more authentic than daytime."

"And so more true?"

"I think so."

"Are you sure?"

"Are you that it's not?"

•　　　•　　　•

Another time Kitty tried interpretation:

"The rocks and bottles you love are broken somehow, right?"

"More or less. What are you asking?"

"Broken like you."

"Hmmm."

"That's too noncommittal. Yes? No? Your paintings are stories of dissolution and grief, images of loss."

"That's smart, but I'm not sure it's true. To me, rocks are just rocks, bottles bottles. Maybe not even that. Excuses for paint, I suspect. Though what paint's an excuse for, I'm not sure."

"But you say you have some obligation to the boulders and driftwood."

"Right. I did pick them up, pick them out. Steal them, if I believe you."

"You have to pay them back?"

"Pay them attention. They're not me. From all I can tell, they're never quite mine. But they let me be interested."

A pause, while Will thought for a moment. "How about—" he said, turning to Kitty, only to discover that she was not looking at him. "How about they're stories of my walks."

She did look up then.

"It's your decision what they are, Will. I'm just asking. Still, why do you walk?"

"To quiet myself, get out of the house. To look."

"But you don't paint what you see. You don't paint landscapes. You don't paint houses. You don't paint cars. People do, you know? You don't even paint the fireplace you stare at all day."

"No, I paint what I find."

"You mean rocks, broken bowls, glasses, and boxes."

"Yes, exactly. Rocks, bowls, glasses, boxes."

"Broken bowls."

"Broken, shards, whatever you want to call them. Broken doesn't mean shattered."

"To make them whole in paint."

"Too smart again, Kitty. You know too much. I used to, but look where it got me. Now I just paint. Yes, I paint broken bowls, glasses, boxes. And I walk. And I don't paint what I see when I walk. And I don't paint the fireplace."

Will knew he was getting defensive, but thought it was time to stop Kitty's desire to give meaning to his life.

"Ever think that you wanted to make your paintings ugly?" Kitty asked.

"Eye of the beholder and all that?"

"I was thinking more of wanting to fail."

"As in beautiful is successful and I'm in a rut and need a therapist?"

"As in making life difficult for yourself and, yes, maybe you do."

"I won't pretend I know much about motive. Maybe you're right. It doesn't really matter."

"What doesn't matter?"

"Why."

"Why not?"

"Because even if I'm trying to frustrate myself, isn't that what I'm after and working for?"

"And the therapist? Or is this your therapy?"

He didn't even try to answer that, or turn to look at her, instead drawing a line in black across his Masonite board, then another in the opposite direction, X-ing out the painting he'd been working on.

•　　　•　　　•

Alone the next day, Will realized she had a point about the fireplace. He'd never thought about the fact that there was little in his paintings to show where he was. Nothing of the room itself, the mantel, or the wall. His backgrounds were anonymous—pale paint that covered the surface behind his still life. For Kitty, Will realized, there was always something there, behind the construction of rocks and wood he created on the table. And because that was true, there was always something missing: the room, his possessions, the surfaces and shapes that as an interior decorator she spent her life altering for herself and others. Will was having enough trouble just concentrating on the rocks themselves to take on more. Still, it was useful to be reminded how blind he was to so much of his world. It was as if the room vanished the moment he started painting inside it. Or maybe when Edie died. Or maybe for the last two decades, as he sat reading or talking with Edie or watching TV.

March 29.

Depth. What we don't understand or know much about when young: depth in life, drawing, family,

*wherever. Maybe depth is not as important as we
pretend, spending (too much) time looking deep,
not enough on the surface. Two dimensions of
canvas, two dimensions to life. Is it depth I look for?
Depth I avoid? The books talk about the illusion of
depth. Which means illusion is enough, that the
stand-in can provide as much as depth might? Does
illusion offer us reality or reassurance?*

Will realized the only bit of furnishings he did
include in his paintings was the table's edge. Sometimes
two edges, front and back. But usually one, sloped, arced,
occasionally almost straight across the line of the canvas.
This too prompted Kitty's attention:

"Do you think about your horizon lines?"

"That's the table, the edge."

"Tabletop, edge, it establishes your horizon line on
the canvas."

"Masonite."

"Whatever, you slug."

"Horizon line like the books talk about, the two-thirds
thing? I was wondering about that, what the instructions
meant. And here I was doing it all along."

She just smiled.

•　　　•　　　•

Another day she tried annoyance:

"On your walks: You don't see people, dogs, cats,
arguments, birds, plants, noises, wind?"

"I do, sometimes, though not as often as you'd
imagine. Or do you want me to say that I see it all in the

boxes and glass, see it reflected in the fingerprints, the discards, the leftovers."

"I don't care what you say, or what you do, you know that. But it's like you're walking through paradise looking at your own toenails."

"Not quite, the paradise. But I like the toenails. Yes. Like when you're on the beach. You can look up to that big horizon and see off to forever. Or you can look down at what's in between your toes, right? The sand, the pebbles, the broken shells. Crab holes sometimes."

"And you're tired of horizons."

"Tired isn't the right word. I'm more interested in something else."

"No more pretty stuff for Mr. You."

"I'm trying to get rid of that pretty/ugly, though I'm not getting far with that. Remember how we laughed at Reagan when he taunted us Sierra Club types by saying that if you've seen one redwood, you've seen them all? That's how I feel now. You look at a sunset—the clouds, the disappearing light, the dark coming on and holding off at the same time. You feel like you could look at it forever. But forever lasts about thirty seconds, usually less, before you turn away, get distracted, start feeling hungry."

"So you stopped looking at them and don't miss them."

"And now I can look down instead, whatever the time of day, and find my toenails."

"Nice speech. No sunsets in toenails."

"Nope."

"No light even."

"That I'm not sure about."

"It's too much for me."

"For me too, sometimes."

"Too little too. Much too little. Pebbles, rocks. You're prehistoric wood yourself. All preserved, all escape."

"Escape? No. I've tried to condemn myself with that word. Did, for a week or two in the fall. But no. Though I'd like to. Escape never has worked for me."

"Contemplation, then. Painting as a form of inaction."

"An admission of boredom maybe."

"You're not bored. Self-satisfied I'd say."

"Not satisfied. Not that. Not yet."

•   •   •

One day, noticing how Will had piled Edie's art books in a corner of the living room, Kitty reminded Will:

"You used to hate art."

"You bet. I still do, mostly."

"But those catalogues in the corner; the three or four open on the floor."

"I have more sitting alongside the bed and open on top of it."

"But you hate it."

"No. I hate art, like in museums, that art."

He stopped his painting for a moment.

"Edie loved exhibits. I still remember the endless trips we'd make to see one show or another, all elbows and chatter. Kids trying to move around faster than their parents, and people asking each other if they liked farm houses better than flowers, haystacks more than guitars."

"Poor sweetie. What an ordeal."

66

"Of course not, next to starvation or homelessness. But yes, actually. I'd walk around trying to be interested, but I saw nothing after three or four paintings."

"There are benches."

"I know every one, would sit as quickly as I could get lost in the people. I'd watch them crowd around a painting, craning their ears into the cassette machines, watch their clothes and the way they'd prop up their bodies while they moved down one wall, then the next."

"Any best moments?"

"Honestly?"

"Why not?"

"If I was lucky, there'd be some women around, who I'd follow from room to room."

"Voyeur."

"There's nothing quite like the swish of hose, you know?"

"I'll remember that."

"Maybe that was worth the time."

"Did Edie know? About the stalking?"

He put down his brush and stared for a few seconds up at the ceiling before smiling.

"Eventually. She figured it out one day, just followed me as I wandered. She got angry, then started teasing me about a hose fetish. Finally, she just shrugged in that way of hers and went back to her paintings or whatever was on exhibit and warned me never ever to open my mouth or pretend to be a feminist."

Will turned to Kitty then.

"She found her own compromise after a while. She'd remind me to pack a book, settle me in the museum café with a glass of wine, and look in every hour or two. You know how it goes—people find ways to live with what they don't like about each other."

"I'm not sure I do know much about that, Will," Kitty said, more serious than usual. "Not the way you two did." She paused, but only for a moment. "But now if you went, you'd have things to notice besides noisy thighs. Or the quality of the wine."

"I think that sometimes, but I don't want to try. I don't want to go inside those buildings to look at the paintings. I wonder if I could see any of them better now. Through the bodies, I mean. I don't think so. I do like the catalogues, though. I'm glad Edie bought so many. It's nice to sit with them, stare at one painting for a long time while I get sleepy. I'm not sure if I learn anything, but I love to stare. That's enough for me."

•   •   •

As March ended, Will had to admit to himself that he was baffled by his efforts as a painter. He knew something was missing—some formula, trick, perception that would help him move forward, progress in that simple childhood sense of getting better the way Helen once did at soccer. Something more than just practice, or repetition. Some logic, or magic. A clue perhaps, that would open a hidden door to a passage as closed to him as the lives he peeked at on his walks.

Over the months, he tried strategy after strategy. His most persistent—and perhaps least successful—began in late winter. He bought a box of throwaway cameras. He'd take several photos of each still life construction he created, and of each canvas as he finished it. His floor was littered with 4x6 color shots as the month went on, but (it seemed to him) to no avail. He would paint over one Masonite or another with gesso, and try to repaint the same construction of rocks, or rocks and driftwood, on the basis of the photos, then put the new painting onto the wall in the slot left by the old, until the walls themselves, living room to entryway to kitchen, became one large, chronologically disordered canvas representing his late winter and early spring.

Hard as he tried to replicate his model, his angle of vision, and his paints, he always found something new to preoccupy him—shadows, or a conversation he thought he could all but overhear between the edge of one rock and the inviting surface of the next. *Why "but"?* he asked himself in his notebook. *Why not glory in what's new? Because nothing holds still and I pretend it should? Evidence of my failure to reproduce what I see vs. discovery of something new to see: is it really that easy a choice?*

However he argued with himself, he grew more and more frustrated by his inability to reconstruct even a semblance of the original rock formations on his table, let alone with paint on the Masonites. He took to outlining his shoes on the living room floor, using different colored markers, and making a note of which day he started each painting so he didn't confuse his position from one day to the next.

The rocks themselves seemed to mock his efforts.

Is it nature that makes them seem so alike to me? Or is it that I'm drawn repeatedly to the same shapes, thicknesses, and colors when I choose rocks? Or is it some failure in my ability to

*distinguish, discriminate, note variation and
difference? Or am I so inept with a brush that I'm
unable to recognize the actual rocks in the still life
from the painting, or the photo of the painting?*

Watching all this, Kitty kept her comments bemused, but polite. "Art is not science," she once noted, as she watched Will's care with a marker on the floor, or the way he kept rearranging his still lifes to get them "right." One day she got up, grabbed a pile of photos from the floor, shuffled them into the order she wanted, and then arranged the rocks the way they once had been. Benny jumped into the game. Quickly, the two of them recreated several more of Will's constructions in empty spots in the living room— "to help," Kitty said to Will's angry looks of surprise at their success. Content with his work, Benny began painting one of the formations that sat near the front door. Will stood frozen in place. He stared at the back of Benny's head, at Kitty, who had returned to her seat with a magazine in her lap, at the little still life models that rested in clumps on the floor. Then back at his own easel and the driftwood and rocks before him on the table.

When Will let out a low moan and threw his brushes down, Kitty looked up.

"At least this tells you that I can recognize the still life from your painting. That's something, Will," Kitty said to him.

"But I can't," he answered before he went into his bedroom, found a jacket, and went to the front door.

"Let yourselves out when Benny's finished. I'll clean up when I get home."

Then he went for a walk.

●　　　　●　　　　●

The only other altercation he had with Kitty came in early April. Benny was asleep in Helen's room. Instead of nestling in a corner with her magazines as usual, Kitty picked up a brush and started painting on Benny's easel. Will stopped his own work and moved alongside her, watching her shame his months of efforts in less than fifteen minutes. When she didn't notice—or ignored— how annoyed he was, he reached over and put his hand on hers, pulling the brush up into the air.

"Edie liked this story about Picasso's dad," he said to Kitty. "He, the dad, was famous for his drawings of doves. When Picasso was fourteen, his father gave him a demonstration of how to draw the birds. Picasso's first drawing was so perfect that his father stopped painting. He kept on teaching, but supposedly never drew or painted again."

"And I'm Picasso."

"Metaphorically. But I won't quit. I'm just telling you how it feels. You can't paint here."

"Because I'm too good, too facile, too fast?"

"Or because I'm not. Any of those. Or I'm too stubborn."

"Or ashamed?"

"Whatever." Here he paused, as if searching for something smart to say. "Or I need to sip my struggles straight."

She laughed at that, reached out a hand to rub his arm in affection. But he pulled back at her touch, so she retreated to her chair and magazines, he to his wall.

●　　　　●　　　　●

Though Will was ready to talk about his painting, his wanderings, and even his garbage-sifting habits with Kitty, he didn't tell her about Nancy. *Hiding something,* he wrote himself. *Box under the bed, rolled-up t-shirt in a drawer, money in the sugar jar: insurance that we're more than others think. Maybe this is what shading tricks bring out, and all that we mean by three dimensions.*

Will came upon Nancy by chance one night in late February. He'd walked by the house many times before. It was one of his favorite wanderings, through the tiny side streets and alleys of the old Seabright area below the rail tracks. When Helen was younger, he and Edie would go there often, to the small beach, or the tiny museum of natural history announced by a huge brass sculpture of a whale that adorned the front. The neighborhood was a tangled mess of tiny one- and two-bedroom cabins built in the 1930s and '40s as summer retreats by people in San Francisco, San Jose, and the Peninsula. Now, with the coming of the university, the jump in property prices, and the obsession with ocean and beach, these uninsulated huts had become unaffordable little gems, planted down firmly on their minuscule half-lots beside the few new ranch-style homes that had managed to get built in the early 1970s. They stood, one beside the next: tiny, no yards, but with the weathered wood exteriors repainted, sometimes retrofitted to support another half-house or ocean-view deck above. The scraps of dirt that passed for yards on front or sides were filled with flowers or an occasional vegetable garden of climbing peas, shade-willing tomatoes, leek, rhubarb, arugula, butter lettuce. These tiny properties dominated the narrow alleyways without sidewalks where Will walked the middle of the street, avoiding the winter and early spring mud on both edges. The little brick museum was backed by a park—a triangle of grass and cypresses that the town had managed to preserve against developer pressure.

And where, one night, Will paused beneath a tree in an increasingly fierce and windy rain to adjust his jacket hood for the couple more miles he imagined wandering before he turned home. He glanced randomly across the spread of grass to the big ranch-style house across the street with a broad picture window. On the right side of the house—his right—a bright living room ended in a doorway. A Mercedes was parked in the driveway in front of a large two-car garage. Will knew from previous visits that a Porsche was often parked alongside. As he stared, a tall thin blond woman crossed the room dressed in what looked like sweat pants and sweatshirt, one hand holding a wine glass, the other a book with a finger inserted in it. She moved to a couch that sat at the back wall of the room. He watched her back as she faced the couch and put her glass and then the book down, open-faced, on an end table. She turned on a lamp, and then turned herself and sat, settling into a comfortable position at the far end of the couch, elbow on the armrest.

It was when she faced him for the first time that Will thought he recognized her as Nancy Cartelli. That possibility made him curious, so he held his position under the tree despite the rain, watching while the woman propped her legs up on a coffee table. She just sat staring out at the weather or park, or perhaps her own reflection in the glass, sipping from the wine, maybe listening to the rain and wind blowing the branches into a clatter that mixed with the heavy pounding of drops on window and gutter.

She must have sat that way for ten minutes, Will thought, staring out in his direction as he stared back at her, before something jumped up onto the couch beside her—a cat, Will decided and confirmed over the next weeks of shameless peeping. She petted the animal, turned to the table beside her, picked up the book, and directed her attention downward to her lap. Will took the opportunity to leave his refuge under the tree, creep closer to the house, stare a while longer through rain-soaked eyes, and decide he'd had enough wandering for one night.

He returned the next night and the one after that. She came into the room about the same time—between midnight and one in the morning—usually with the book and wine glass as on that first evening. Twice, there were fires in the fireplace that she'd get up occasionally to extend with a new log. Often her time would begin with standing at the window itself, staring out—looking at nothing in particular, Will decided. Just standing there, a book and wine glass in her hands. Once, she carried a few magazines or catalogues—something glossy—instead of the book; once a pile of newspapers, and sat with a pen or pencil in hand. Another night, she brought an opened bottle of wine along with the glass, and worked her way through about a third of it before she reversed herself—got up, tamped the fire, put out the table lamp, picked up the book, wine glass and bottle. Then as he watched, she moved across to the wide arc of doorway that seemed to lead to some hall or bedrooms hidden to his view, where she snapped a switch and turned the room dark, just a sliver of some other light reaching out into it from back in her life. By then, usually, it was two, sometimes even three or four a.m., and Will turned for home and bed himself. Even after that first week's watch, after he returned to his garbage scavenging, he visited Nancy regularly—on Thursdays when her garbage got put out, and at least one night each weekend. He usually found her there, as devoted to her time in the corner of the sofa as he was to his in the dark seclusion of the trees.

•   •   •

Nor did he tell Kitty about Jess until much later—not, in fact, until after she had returned from time away, the impatient gesture of the traveler who couldn't stay put for long.

It was mid-April when she left, carrying Benny along with her to Boston where the boy's mother and father were, as Kitty put it, "trying to make a go of it." Kitty planned to head from there down to New York to meet with some stores about a line of colorful brooms and fans she was importing, before she picked up the boy again to take him with her on a tour of New Mexico ("The Southwest thing is done on the big scale, but that's when you really find the secret caches. There's money being the latecomer.")

As a remembrance, Will offered Benny three small rocks he knew the boy liked—rocks Will himself had once cherished. He and the boy decided they resembled a bison, a dog, and a bat. And so Terron, Tremble, and Tot were born. A story about them came slowly, a rendering of Montana tall grass plains Will had never seen, where Terron (the bison) lived on long after the herds had disappeared, where Tremble (the dog) befriended the bison one day after chasing him into a cave and nearly causing the galloping animal to break a leg when he fell in his fear, a cave where Tot (the bat) hung out all day in dark solitude until his nightly rounds. It is Tot who unwittingly leads Tommy, the homeless town boy who survives as he can in a little tin shack by the deserted quarry, back to the cave one night when the boy spots the bat against the moonlit sky and sets out in stealthy pursuit. It is Tommy who names, and slightly tames, the three creatures. And who, despite his precautions, is himself followed to their lair by Switch Holcomb, the town bully. Switch hates Tommy, and is armed with a big stick ready to hurt the boy. But when Switch sees Terron lounging at the mouth of the cave along with Tommy and the bat, he expands his ambitions, determined to kill the bison, capture the bat, and torture Tommy. But Switch doesn't notice Tremble the dog, who is quietly tracking him.

At which point Will stopped, as he did often with Helen, insisting that this was enough for now, promising that he would tell more when Benny sent him stories of his own travels. He handed the three rocks over to Benny with ritualistic formality, eliciting a promise that the boy would protect the little rock animals and wrap them carefully in his backpack.

Will himself, meantime, was starting to realize that he too was being followed. He had just finished his time picking through trash along Walk Circle, and had moved onto Woodrow—a vast, wide thoroughfare that ended at the water and had once been a landing strip for small planes—when he heard someone running behind him, and Jess Arnold appeared at his side, panting.

"What were you doing there?" the boy asked when he caught his breath.

Will, surprised and embarrassed, not sure yet if he'd been caught in the act, tried to evade the question with ones of his own, along with a false pleasure at seeing his former student again months after their encounter at the Tracery.

Jess was persistent. "I saw you. The garbage cans. The bottle you've got in your backpack. The flashlight."

Will tried to just walk away then. They walked two more blocks towards the ocean, Will hoping his impolite silence would unsettle the boy so he'd give up.

Jess just kept pace, quietly.

Finally, Will surrendered, pulled the bottle he'd just acquired out of his pack and handed it wordlessly to Jess to examine as the two of them continued to walk towards the beach.

"I've been watching you for the last three weeks," Jess admitted, when they got to the beach and Will looked at him in the pale light of a half-moon.

"I guess you didn't know I was following. I thought it was you, but wasn't sure at first, so I've been tracking you here and there, Westside, Eastside, Seabright, Westlake."

"What are you doing out at night?" Will asked.

"Just restless. Can't sleep sometimes. I just get up and walk. I like the town at night."

"I know the feeling. You walk all over? Just by yourself?"

"Yeah. Or I did. Until I saw you. You walk a lot."

Will looked at him then, annoyed to realize how oblivious he had been.

"I didn't mean anything," Jess said. "Just curious. I wanted to see what you were after."

Will paused then, unsure if he wanted to go on to ask the next thing that popped into his head.

"You saw me in the park in front of your house?"

The boy hesitated.

"It's not my house. It's my stepdad's. And my mom's."

"You've watched me there."

"Yeah. That's where it started, in the park. I like to watch her too."

"Nancy? Your mother?"

Jess nodded.

"Yeah. She seems so quiet then, peaceful. Like there's nothing to do, ever, but read and sit and sip wine. It makes me think she's happy."

"But she isn't?"

Jess didn't say anything again for a few seconds before he turned the question back to Will.

"Are you?"

Which stopped Will's curiosity for the moment, and began their unspoken partnership. Will never knew when the boy would appear, but appear he did, almost every weeknight or morning; sometimes at one, sometimes as late as three. Sometimes it was while Will stood in the park looking at Nancy. Will would feel some presence near him, glance into the shadows, and sees the boy's outline, quietly standing or sitting on a patch of grass maybe ten feet away. They would nod at each other, say nothing, turn back to the house. Eventually, maybe a half hour later, one would start to move, the other follow, though sometimes the boy stayed on as Will drifted off down the street.

Mostly Jess appeared as Will wandered one neighborhood or another in what he had until then thought was an impromptu and unpredictable series of decisions on his part. Jess ambled alongside for an hour or more, with little to offer of conversation or advice. It amazed, even frightened, Will a bit to see how Jess managed to find him even when Will deliberately worked to alter his habits, travel a new route, vary his routine. Whatever he thought to do, the boy would appear. His own desire to avoid Jess's companionship waned as he realized that Jess was not going away—was as persistent as Kitty, in fact, and as irresistible. So Will stopped trying to protect himself. Eventually he realized that he looked forward to the inevitable moment when he heard footsteps and felt the boy beside him, matching his stride, his intentional lack of intention, his silence.

There was something in Jess's quiet that Will found soothing. It was as if the boy were there and not at the same time—the one figure Will could remember in a long while who asked nothing of him. Until the day he did.

•   •   •

With Kitty and Benny gone, Will found he was completing a painting every three days. One painting stopped him for almost a week, for reasons he didn't understand. The rocks he chose were familiar ones: a long, angular piece like a broken arrowhead that sat horizontally on the bed sheet that covered his dining room table; three round humps that he set up in a line behind; a fifth rock that was like movie icebergs nestled in back of those so it resembled a mountain rising stark behind low hills, the hills pushed up against it as if before a hidden, undulating valley. But somehow, whatever he did to adjust his lighting, the texture of each plane broke in complex ways across the others. Will realized he hadn't the faintest idea how to reproduce anything resembling the particulars, let alone the emotional feel, of the scene before him.

> *Kitty insists art classes would help, but don't*
> *want that. Does that mean I don't want to*
> *improve? Yes and no, as usual. Does mean my*
> *art's private, like a mistress, sin—cross-dressing,*
> *binge eating, porno films. I want to paint*
> *without words attached (what are these?).*
> *Without advice maybe.*

He had to admit that he missed Kitty. Her disappearance once again, despite the ways he had encouraged—or at least not resisted—her departure, made him feel abandoned. He recognized that he was irascible and suspicious when she was around; still, he persisted in thinking that she had run out on him. Her four postcards—postmarked on three consecutive Wednesdays, the last a two-card delivery—made him imagine she wrote him the way some couples wound up the grandfather clock each week, or screwed on a given day, or took out the garbage. Still each time he'd eat his nightly salads or bowls of soup, he found himself looking at the cards sitting on the kitchen counter, collecting bits of food:

> Taos is Peckinpah gone genteel. Adobe and tiles
> and pickup trucks with guns mounted on the
> back windows. And galleries inside jewelry
> shops inside t-shirt stores inside rug dealers
> inside galleries. More jewelry than arms and
> fingers to wear them. All the large stones on

wrists and necks and ears make me tired of blue
and green. But better than Boston was:
Samantha feisty and defensive, her shoulders
straddling her ears when hubby in the room.
Benny was confused. Me too. We're both
quieter now.

The next one was more temperate:

Time to myself (with B) to wander the mountain
trails. Lugged B along from one studio to next,
found some old guys here, lefty artists, still
banging away at their sculptures and oils in their
80s. Fighting old fights too like the '30s weren't
history. Like you should be. More later.

And then the last one—or actually, two—numbered, the
same picture of saguaro cactus on the front as the others,
but with more details:

Spent day with sculptor, 89. Took to Benny and
had him pounding metal in his studio while B
told him about your rocks, bison and bat. Acres
of empty land around worn-out mess of a
house: barn with kiln, fiberglass-roofed area,
his sculptures scattered over the grounds like a
museum garden. Refugee from NYC. Some of
his work uglier than yours, but he sells his.

Then on the first card, followed without salutation or
signature by the second:

When his wife died, he turned her hair into art
piece: a dangling wig hanging on an upside-down

'L' arm of fiberglass with swear words along the arm in a rainbow of colors. Her hair brush is sticking through the thin follicles of the wig like they're being combed, forever. A photo of his face at one end, arranged so her hair resembles a long tongue. He's got a new lover. She's in her 60s, warm, friendly, quiet. Seems to ignore his rants. Rest of his stuff less perverse, maybe also less interesting.

He missed Benny too, who sent him five short postcards—each with a picture on the front. The first was a crayon drawing of what he assumed were Benny's mother and father, both stunted in height; one on each side of an equally tall Benny with a big round hole in his face filled with rows of bright teeth. They were each holding one of the boy's hands while they stared straight ahead.

The back read, "Daddy and Mommy meet me at the airport." This was followed by two more with similar drawings—"Mommy and Daddy and me eating hot dogs," "Mommy and Daddy and me at a baseball game," and then a fourth with the same three figures covered in light blue over swim trunks and bare legs: "Mommy and Daddy and me in the pool."

The fifth was of a woman—he imagined it as Benny's version of Kitty—with a paintbrush in her hand standing next to what he took to be an old man. The man was using some hammer-like instrument to bang on one side of an indecipherable shape—a nascent bear in hibernation? a boulder?—while a child figure bigger than the adults held up an even larger hammer. The position of the woman's paintbrush and the old man made it seem like the woman had just finished painting the man into existence. On the back, the story: "Gran and me working with Hank in his studio making a production."

As promised, Will would sit down and write back segments of a story to Benny. By this time, Terron, Tremble, Tot, and Tommy had survived three dangerous attacks from Switch Holcomb. Tremble had become a skilled tracker, his dog nose glued to the ground to catch a whiff of intruders. Tot the bat had learned to read Tremble's slightest whines for signs of disturbance—and had even once engaged a host of other bats deeper in the cave to help frighten Switch away. Terron, meanwhile, roamed the grasses alongside Tommy, who had learned to ride the huge beast and clean its hide with a makeshift comb he'd created from discarded fishhooks. Switch's last and most dangerous attack included a group of thugs, the Switcheroos. But the animals outsmarted the gang by leading the bullies into a maze they devised in the tall prairie grass that eventually deposited the teens at the town garbage dump and a meeting with the gnats who swarmed there. Will found himself pleased with his new array of characters, though straining to imagine what came next. He wondered too whether the Benny who returned (if he returned) would be ready for a new set of heroes.

He hadn't seen Jess in a few nights—more than a week, in fact—which worried Will enough to wander by the art store late one weekend afternoon. Jess was helping a woman and child, retrieving something from behind the counter. When he looked up, he saw Will staring at him. He stared back for a full five seconds, but he offered no smile in return, or nod, or lift of a hand. Then he turned his attention back to the woman and boy. Will moved off and returned home to his own work and to his nightly solitude—rebuffed perhaps, or not curious enough, or just quiet enough inside his own habits to let Jess figure out what was going on without prying questions.

4

I T WAS FOUR IN THE MORNING when Will returned from his nightly walk. As he trudged up the wooden steps to the back deck, he felt broken glass through the soles of his shoes. He saw more glass at the edge of the French doors that led to the kitchen. Two panes alongside the door handle were empty; small shards still stuck in the wooden muntin. He crept inside carefully, less worried about confronting someone than curious what anyone might steal. There was a gap along the wall where two Masonite panels—two of Will's paintings that hung among a dozen others on the wires strung horizontally along the wall— were missing. A folded piece of paper hung in their place.

> Sorry I've disappeared on you. But I suppose I
> don't need to apologize for secrecy to you, do I?
> I'm leaving town tonight. I'm pretty sure my

stepdad knows about Mom. He's been trying to get stuff out of me. He hits her, I think, but she says no. That's why I watch, even though watching doesn't do any good. But since you watch her too, watch her for me. And please help her.

Sorry about the window. I took three of the bottles I remember from when we hunted together. And two paintings. I'll keep them safe.

I liked our walks. You know how to be quiet and I don't know anyone but Mom and me who does.

Jess

Then two short postscripts:

Your house is weird for a teacher. For anyone.

I'll write when I can.

The letter in one hand, Will stared at the empty space on the wall. He walked into his living room and looked at the bottles and other pieces of glass and plastic piled haphazardly alongside the windows. He could imagine they had been disturbed. Maybe. Except for the note, the absent windowpanes, and the space along the wall, nothing else had changed. But he felt like he'd just lived through an earthquake. Jess Arnold had broken in and brought something new into his life. Or taken something away. His ex-student Jess—someone who walked alongside him for hours, or used to; a boy as unabrasive as a worn dish towel—stole two paintings and two worthless bottles. And gave Will the job of watching over his mother.

Will cut a piece of cardboard and taped it over the hole in the doorway, then circled his rooms for the next two hours. He made a pot of coffee and ate some tasteless cereal. He climbed up to his roof, where he hadn't been for weeks, but that brought no relief.

When midnight came, Will took off as he always did on his round of walking. He forced himself to maintain his routine, moving aimlessly from street to street. Three or four hours of wandering brought him to the park outside Nancy's windows. She sat in her living room as usual, though she seemed restless to his newly informed, if confused, eye. She'd sit, pick up a magazine, stare at it for a few minutes, then take up another. She picked up a book, but just let it lay in her lap while she stared up from the pages. Her cat jumped up alongside her on the couch, but she pushed it onto the floor every time it tried to sit on her lap. She stood up, sat down, stood up again. She walked to the large glass window at the front of the house, turned around, then turned back, as if looking for something she couldn't find. Standing at his spot in the park across the way, under the diffuse light from stars and moon, Will remembered how often he stood just like Nancy at his own front window during the last weeks Edie was alive and the first days after she died, inattentive, frozen in place.

When Will returned to his vantage point the next night, and the one after that, Nancy was gone. The house was dark. Two cars were parked in the driveway, but without Nancy at her nightly station—wine glass on the side table, cat alongside—there was nothing to see. Swearing to himself, Will headed home.

By the third day after Jess's break-in, Will was back at work. Questions kept gnawing at him, but he fought them off, determined not to let the boy's disappearance alter the pattern of his life, while knowing full well that it already had. He dug into fewer garbage cans than usual on his walks and spent less time staring into the houses that he passed. His walks inevitably led him back to the park and to Nancy's house, but there was nothing to see. The house seemed tranquil, quiet, hidden, a world unto itself.

He struggled with his frustrations in his notebook:

Life getting cluttered with people spoiling the view. Didn't feel empty before but stuffed now. Constipated. I need prunes or a more unpopulated diet. Or I need to control my own need to taste the minds of others.

What is it about isolation that makes people want to enter and so end it? Is it like punching a hole in a vacuum, letting in air, to escape the emptiness? Are painting and collecting bottles and cans and bowls ways of restoring air to the vacuum, or maintaining this insulation I claim as mine? If they are my way to claim independence, why and how have I drawn other people into my solitary habits?

•   •   •

Nancy appeared at Will's front door eight days after Jess's break-in. She announced herself with a soft, persistent knocking late in the morning. Will had just finished breakfast and was moving to his easel. He peeked out at Nancy, her body turned sideways away from the house, one hand extended to the door while the other clutched a cardigan around her thin frame. Her shoulders were sloped inward, as if protecting herself from something. She looked tentative, worried, thin-lipped; her hand in a fist holding clumps of the thick sweater. A piece of paper stuck out of her left hand. When he opened the door, he thought he sensed some pleading in her. Later he realized that their whole conversation took place while the two of them barely moved from their positions: she standing on the small porch, the sweater clutched around her; he a step above, at the edge of the threshold. The morning fog had not yet lifted, and the smell of ocean, mist, and something a little rank still hung in the morning air.

"I'm looking for Jess."

"He's not here."

"I guessed he wasn't. He told me to come here. Emailed me."

"I don't know where he is."

"But you know something."

Will wasn't sure what he knew.

"He was here, about a week ago. I didn't see him. He broke in."

She looked alarmed.

"He took some things. Nothing important. Not to me anyway."

He paused.

"He left me a note. It said he was leaving town."

"That's all?"

Will paused again.

"He said he thought he was in trouble. That you were in trouble."

"What's that to you?"

She didn't deny the trouble, Will noticed.

"Jess's email said you know everything. What do you know?"

Will was thrown back on his ignorance.

"Jess said he was scared. Talked about your husband."

"They don't get along."

"I used to walk around town late at night with Jess. We'd wander from one street to another."

"He's always been like that," she said, with what Will thought was pride.

Nancy stared down at the note in her hand, and again asked: "What do you know?"

Will decided he owed Nancy something for all his nights of staring at her.

"Jess and I used to watch you. From the park in front of your house."

He saw that the information startled her. She turned to face him more directly—confrontational, but still slope-shouldered, still holding Jess's email crumpled in her hand.

"Watching what?"

"Nothing really. We would sit in the park. You were in your house. We watched you sip wine, read, pet your cat. What you do late at night. Nothing special."

She paused, turning away from him, taking in this information like it was something new she was learning about herself.

"How long?"

"I don't know how long for Jess. A few weeks? He's worried about you."

"And you? Are you worried too?" she asked.

"Yes. No. Not at first. I walk at night, like Jess. I have since Edie died. I can't sleep. I walk."

She didn't say anything.

"You looked so quiet. I didn't think I was hurting anyone."

"You had no right."

"No. I had no right. I'm sorry. You looked peaceful. I didn't see anything. Really. Just you sitting and reading." He paused for a moment, then added, "I'm also discreet."

At that she started to cry and shake, further crumpling the piece of paper in her hand. He thought to hold her, thought to leave her and find some Kleenex, thought to say something. But instead he just stood where he was.

"You had no right, Mr. Moran. No right. No right. I'm sorry for your loss. Your wife. She was a good person. You were too. Are. Helped me that year … were one of the ones who didn't … look down on me."

He nodded.

"I'm sorry you're lonely. But I'm not a show."

"I know."

She was quiet for a moment. "Jess told me to come to you for help. But you can't help. No one can." She looked up at him then. "You're not my teacher anymore." She paused. "I need to find Jess."

With that, Nancy turned away and walked slowly down the steps, her upper body folded forward at the waist as she struggled to hold herself upright.

Will closed the door and went to his front window, with its white tarp acting as curtain. He pulled aside a slit and stared at Nancy while she crossed the street to the Mercedes that he'd seen parked in her driveway night after night. She closed the car door, then sat crying for a good two minutes more before she started the engine and drove off, never once looking back at Will's house.

Which left Will to examine his prowling habits in his notebook:

> *The tortures of living, absence, worry, love.*
> *Peeking at neighbors: old bras, tired bodies.*
> *Everyday rock and roll. So much attention to so*
> *little—kids, depression, tomato plants, what to*
> *wear to work. Was life with Edie anything else?*
> *But the melodrama, Nancy with her tears, me*
> *with nothing to offer but news that she'd been*
> *spied on by a Peeping Tom and her son. Absent*
> *son. All so banal. Shared at how many front*
> *doors today? Sad as garbage cans. Or old men*
> *who dig in them.*

Will was ashamed—ashamed of his peeks into Nancy's life, into windows all over town, into garbage. He realized he hadn't actually talked to Nancy since she came up to him to offer condolences at Edie's funeral last June. And in the two or more years before that, their talks were only about the business of food delivery: a call from her the last Sunday of every month to reassure him that there would be dinners waiting on the front porch. He thanked her, she dismissed his thanks, he thanked her again, they hung up. Every so often he and Edie would send her a gift—

he remembered placemats, a fancy bell-pull Edie bought on a trip to France that sat in its original packing for years. In all that time, when worry touched most things he said, Nancy's voice remained upbeat, confident, in a way he never remembered her being as a teenager, or in his parent-teacher conferences when he taught her twin boys. Her voice now, at his front door, haunted Will for days afterwards, the strain and ache of it like a piece of wayward chalk on a blackboard.

•　　　•　　　•

After Nancy's visit, Will scrupulously circled away from her neighborhood as if it had been condemned. The nights felt less amiable to him, less quietly accepting. It was a relief, he realized, when he heard a tentative rapping at his door about five one morning. He had just returned from his wandering and was readying himself for bed. The fog hovered over everything, though when he opened the door, he noticed the sky was appreciably lighter than it had been just ten minutes before.

It was Nancy again, less steady on her feet. She was wearing the same cardigan as a week before, but this time over a sweatshirt and pants like the ones Will was familiar with from his weeks of watching her. Her face was tear-stained, though it was the bruises and raw flesh he first noticed and not the tears.

He looked quickly to the street, didn't see her car parked anywhere, wondered idly how she got here, and wondered if she had been standing somewhere across the way awaiting his return. This time he did leave the doorway, walked out onto the small porch and reached one arm protectively to her shoulder to steer her into the house. She resisted, so he instead led her to the top steps, where he sat her down and sat down next to her.

Her face was ashen and full of colors: ochre, plum, carnelian. Soft reds blended into purples and yellows. Dried blood trailed from an edge of her lip. Crusts of darker red clogged beneath her nose, which had swollen, turned bulbous, a faint brown. She sat there for what seemed like several minutes, not saying a word, her breath coming through clenched lips and making a huffing sound as it pushed out her blood-darkened nose. When she did speak, it was softly, a kind of croaking, like she didn't want to say what she did, or like she hadn't quite awakened yet and her voice was still thick with the darkness.

"I think I need that help now, Mr. Moran."

"Of course. And it's Will."

She tried to nod at that, but the muscles in her neck must have hurt because all she wound up doing was biting her lip.

"Just a couple nights. A place to stay. Dave drinks too much. He sometimes hits me."

"This has happened before."

"Not this. A little. Nothing."

"Jess thought he was hurting you."

"I guessed he thought that. It wasn't anything. Really. Dave doesn't want to hurt me. Or didn't." She paused for a moment, as if listening to what she had just said. "But he knows. Dave that is. About …"

She trailed off and rubbed her hand along the thin streak of blood that had dried at the edge of her mouth.

Will reached into his store of clichés: "About you being with someone else."

Her eyes registered surprise, though the rest of her face only moved slightly, as if shaking from a chill.

"Yes. He's always been jealous. Protective, I liked to say."

Her voice trailed off again.

"Nothing to be jealous about," she went on. "Until Ken."

Will left those details for the moment.

"And he did this tonight."

She nodded.

"Where is he now?"

"I don't know. He left. I was crying, on the bed. I heard him break something—a lamp in the hall. Then the car started. He likes to drive at night."

"When he's drinking."

"All the time. Fast. 'Time for the highway,' he'll say."

She paused. "He's careful. Never DUI; never even gotten a ticket. He's proud of that."

She paused again.

"Always comes home. Tender, wanting me. Ready with a washcloth."

Another short pause.

"And jewelry the next day."

She smiled slightly, as if this were the first time she'd made the connection.

"And you left."

She nodded.

"And walked here?"

"It isn't far."

At least three miles, mostly uphill, Will knew.

She started to shake. Will got up, went to his bedroom and came back with a blanket that he wrapped around her. Then he went back into the house, filled a bowl with cool water and found a clean towel. He sat next to her, patting her face with the towel while she whimpered when he touched a raw spot. He kept patting and rinsing, returning to the kitchen for clean water. She held the blanket around her, shaking still, silent except for her tiny cries. He asked once if she wanted to talk, she just shook her head no. It was only after he returned the bowl and towel to the kitchen the third time that he roused her. She didn't resist, seemed oblivious as they walked through the living room with its easel and still life, walls of paint and floor full of rocks into the back hallway, and down the hallway to Helen's room.

He put her to bed on the mattress that sat on the floor. He tucked her into the large comforter that sat in a heap atop the mattress, curling the sides around her, cocoon-like. When her shivering continued, he grabbed the blanket off his own bed and wrapped that around her as well. Then he let himself down on the worn rug alongside the mattress, his butt pushing up dust as he sat. He realized, distractedly, that he hadn't vacuumed in months, though Nancy seemed indifferent to everything but whatever it was she was staring at on the empty white ceiling. He sat awkwardly on his knees and put his arms around hers outside the covers.

She glanced at him for a moment, and just as quickly returned to her vigil on the ceiling. Gradually, feeling his own knees and back aching from the odd position, and uncomfortable with his intimacies, he moved away and just sat next to her, one hand resting on her shoulder. He felt her shaking slow, replaced by some twitches, little jolts that crossed her cheek as she quieted. She slumped down, turned away from him and curled into herself on her side. Her eyes closed, twitched, closed again, and her breathing eased.

Just as he was sure she was asleep, she sat up suddenly, turned to him, and said her son's name.

"Jess?"

"I haven't heard from him."

She nodded, as if prepared for that answer, and slipped back onto the mattress, her back once again to Will.

Will waited a few more minutes, then found himself a blanket and lay down on his bed.

5

IT WASN'T VERY LONG after Will put Nancy to bed when the banging began, followed by the sound of breaking glass. By the time he got through the hall, he saw Nancy already at the front door, hand on knob. She was wearing the same workout pants and sweatshirt, but now also a towel wrapped turban-like around what he immediately realized must be wet hair from a shower. She had barely turned the door handle before a large man dressed in a white shirt and dark blue business suit burst in, pushing Nancy across the narrow space into the wall behind, screaming:

"Where the fuck is he? Huh? Where's the bastard?"

Before Nancy could answer, the man turned into the living room, where Will stood in his boxers, jeans in one hand.

Will expected Dave to rush him, but instead the man stopped where he was for a second in surprise, then turned to Nancy.

"This? This old turd? You were fucking around with this piece of trash?"

Then he moved towards Will, who stood in a daze, tensed against the attack he felt sure was coming. What came was a fist to his jaw that turned his head to the left and sent him spinning. He watched himself fall sideways, awkwardly, onto the hand that still held his jeans, the knuckles making contact with the floor before his head hit the edge of one of his rock piles. Without much force, he realized, as he tried to push himself up.

In the midst of the fall, he heard Nancy screaming at her husband:

"No. Dave. Stop. It's not him. It's not him. He's my old teacher."

By then Dave was standing over Will, crouched now on all fours shaking his head to try to clear his attention.

"Yeah? I can just imagine what he tried to teach you, you stupid slut."

Dave kicked up while he talked. The toe of his shoe hit Will in the stomach and lifted him slightly so he felt the weight leave his arms and legs, though they still touched the floor. As he registered the pain, he collapsed sideways and fell against the uneven surface of a rock hill. Will noticed the easel on the floor in front of him, one wooden leg cracked. He heard a pounding above his head and looked up to see Nancy standing there, a heavy piece of driftwood in both hands, banging it down on Dave's shoulders and back until her burly husband turned away from Will, grabbed it from her, and flung it across the room, where it smashed into pieces against another pile of rocks.

At this, Dave looked around for a moment, and almost stuttered in his rage.

"What the hell is this? A graveyard? Who the hell lives here?"

And with that, he lurched away from Will, down the hall, crashing open one door after another, his fists and body banging along both sides of the passageway. Will heard the sound of glass breaking, of drawers pulled out, of piles of clothing or towels (something soft) hitting the floor. The decrescendo of banging reversed and grew louder, urging Will to more intense efforts to stand. He saw Dave again as he moved out of the hallway, cardboard sheets of Benny's artwork in his fists and strewn on the floor behind. The man slipped on something as he came up alongside Will once more, paused to regain his balance, and smashed his knee into Will's side while Nancy tried to pull him away.

Dave glanced at his wife then, laughed, smashed her open-palmed across her lips and snarled, "What a dump! Same sort of shit you used to live in. Can't get it out of your system?"

He picked her up then, and dropped her onto Will, lying sideways across the rock pile. Nancy's weight hit him along the sides of his stomach and ribs, so he again collapsed to the floor.

"Well, enjoy it, you dumb whore!" Dave screamed at her.

He tried to turn away, but got his legs tangled in Nancy's while she flayed him with her fists and struggled to get up. Dave kicked at her then, lifting one leg then the other high enough to free it and headed out of the room, across the entry, to the kitchen in the back of the house.

From where he lay at the edge of the rock pile, Will looked up at Nancy, who was simultaneously crying and yelling Dave's name to his departing back. He couldn't see well, sweat or tears fogging his eyes. But he saw a red blotch across her cheek and chin where Dave had slapped her, and felt her hands on his arm as she braced to push herself up. Once her weight was off him, he, too, tried to rise, but slowly, first onto his knees, then carefully putting one leg then the other beneath him, holding onto the rocks for support.

Nancy had started to rush away after Dave, but seeing Will's tentative efforts, she came back, offered a hand under one shoulder, and got him standing. He smiled at her, she nodded, then turned back to the kitchen. Will heard breaking glass from that direction, then the sound of his back door crashing closed. The redwood deck banged with Dave's steps, then Will could hear another door (he guessed the shed) opening and more things heaved up or down or at a wall.

By this time, Nancy was trying to open the back door. He was a dozen feet behind, holding on to a strip of Masonites while he pushed himself slowly along. Nancy was screaming Dave's name, and the word "please" over and over, her voice muffled by the tears that seemed almost to convulse her where she stood in the open doorway, unable or unwilling to move out of the house itself. Then there was a moment of quiet, a door banging shut outside, and one last shout from Dave:

"Slut! Garbage! Cunt! Stupid! Stupid! Stupid!" he yelled.

He must have fallen, Will thought, because he heard a growl and the man swearing at himself. Then his heavy steps again, banging unevenly down the driveway.

The silence in Dave's wake lasted less than five minutes while Will stood where he was, one arm extended to the wall, supporting himself with his palm, listening to Nancy cry. He heard a crackling noise that came from outside and slowly pulled himself along the wall. Nancy was kneeling in the doorway, her back against an edge of the frame, her legs folded up, her arm covering her head.

She looked up as he came even with her. Will looked down at her face, a ravaged mixture of resignation, apology, questioning, despair—he wasn't sure what he saw, even days later, when he tried to recreate the moment. Then she too must have heard the crackling, because Will saw all those sentiments disappear as she jumped up and turned to the back shed. Through the cracked window panes, he could see smoke and bits of flame.

As they both watched, they heard a crashing sound of something hitting the floor, and a burst of yellow flashed up inside the small building. Will turned for the phone. He heard Edie's voice then, suddenly, from out of nowhere, her years of admonition and warning about the flammable contents couched as aphorism: "That shed's a Fourth of July waiting for independence, Will. Wonder what will set it free?" "Fourth of July"—one of those Edieisms he'd lived with so long they lost meaning. Until now.

Before he could move, he heard the sound of a siren growing louder outside. So he went over to Nancy, said "Fire," and stood there with her, watching the blaze through the shed's window and doorway, where the glass had shattered from the heat.

It was Nancy who pulled him back inside and held him up under one arm as she helped him into his jeans. Once dressed, he started back to the phone, but Nancy put her hand over his, stopped him from picking it up and shook her head.

Will resisted, looking at her.

"You don't want him arrested," he said.

"No. Please."

Will started to protest, but she again pushed the phone down onto its base and put her other hand on his lips, insisting on silence.

She took his hand and led him out the front door and down the steps. A small group of curious neighbors in jeans, jackets, aprons, and shorts had already assembled at the bottom of the driveway. The small congregation stared at the two of them—him in jeans and shirt, her in her sweatsuit—as they moved across the weedy front lawn. Will looked at his watch: 3:30 p.m.

Through the next hours, Nancy said nothing to him that he could remember—just nodded, smiled, held onto and supported him. She smiled to his neighbors and politely replied to their questions while Will moved off from her now and then to a position at a convenient tree, where he worked to hold himself up. His stomach and ribs hurt, and he couldn't take a deep breath. He stared back at his house and the smoke and fire emerging over the rooftop, a musty cloud that slowly ascended into the air and down to him along the driveway in the gradually fading light.

It didn't take the fire department long to end the blaze, leaving a charred wooden rectangle of boards and wet ash where the shed once stood. It was Nancy who handled the police when they arrived; explained how she was over trying to help Mr. Moran clean out his shed after his wife's death, how they had lit an old kerosene lamp out there at one point and thought they had extinguished it, but must not have when they went inside for some tea. The neighbors said that they had heard yelling and broken glass; that, she said, was a TV on too loud; Mr. Moran was a little hard of hearing.

Will listened quietly, nodding confirmation when asked, saying little himself, struck by the absurdity of the story but holding back, waiting for instructions. He thought about Jess, and wondered if the boy would consider Will's silence a way to help Nancy, or leave her more vulnerable. But he felt tired, bone-tired, dead tired, unwilling or unable to intervene.

Fortunately, the police never went inside the house itself to observe the damage or look for a TV. Maybe they believed Nancy's tale; maybe they didn't, but had other calls awaiting them. Maybe they too were ready to be convinced, or were too smart to believe a word, but too bored to need to uncover surprises. Maybe they knew the neighborhood well enough to know that Will, or some family that he was part of, had lived here quietly for years, and that was enough evidence for them. Maybe they figured whatever domestic scene had taken place was best left unnoticed since neither of the adults seemed upset. No one, Will realized later, noticed or at least cared about the bruises on Nancy's face. When Will thought back to the night, he realized she'd artfully covered much of her lower jaw with the towel that had been around her hair when Dave first came into the house. He wondered later if she was practiced at such evasion.

An accident, so the paper reported a couple days later. Which was almost true, Will had to admit. The fire part anyway. Retired teacher loses shed full of old keepsakes.

Will had to ward off several former colleagues who came by offering consolation, no doubt curious about the young woman they caught sight of working alongside Will cleaning up the damage. But they were used to his querulous silence, and didn't seem to care enough to insist on more than a passing attempt at sympathy.

●　　　●　　　●

Little remained of the shed or Will's boxes. What was left was covered by wet soot. For the next several days, Will gave up his painting, working instead to rid himself of the acrid smell and black residue of wood and cardboard, old toys and outgrown children's clothes, charred pebbles, burnt-out paint cans and scraps of photographs. In a little more than a week, the hubbub settled down; in three, the blackened ruins were swept away, leaving just a darkened concrete slab to remind Will what he and Edie had been storing there.

By then, Nancy had taken up residence in Will's house and bedroom. Only temporarily, they both understood, without the subject of time coming up formally between them. Neither returned to bed the night of the fire. Once the clamor of firemen, police, and neighborhood curiosity died down, they silently worked hauling away trash, and fixed a quick midnight meal of canned soup they consumed standing at the kitchen counter. They took an hour off for Will to drive Nancy to her home.

Will used the car ride to bring up Dave again, afraid for his own safety as well as hers.

"He won't be there," she confidently explained. "He'll be driving."

"And if he is?"

"I won't go in."

"Why wouldn't you let me call the cops?"

Nancy shrugged her shoulders. Will let the silence carry them a few blocks more before she said, "I love Dave. He's my husband. He's good to me. Or used to be. He's a good lawyer, helps people. He helped me when I needed it, helped me turn my life around. If the cops get him, his career's over. I think he's always known that, and he keeps drinking and driving drunk anyway."

"And hitting you. And burning down buildings and kicking people."

"He won't do that again, any of it; that I know. I won't let him."

"But you can't stop him. Couldn't, tonight."

"Didn't try, tonight. Or tried too late. Tonight wasn't Dave," she said, looking up at Will. "He found out about this stuff."

"Your affair."

Nancy nodded. "Yeah. My pathetic affair."

Will waited to see if she'd go on, but she didn't.

"If he's hit you before, and he's as jealous as you say, he's going to come after you."

She seemed to consider that for a minute.

"No. At least I don't think so. I need to see a lawyer. Get a restraining order."

"And that will stop him?"

"It will if he doesn't want to lose his license." Then she laughed. "Anyway, it's clear you can't stop him, so why don't you let me take over?"

Will wasn't quite ready to let her off with a slight at his manhood. "I'd trust the cops more."

"I wouldn't. It's my life, so stay out of this."

Nancy's ferocity surprised Will and even seemed to surprise Nancy herself for a moment.

"I'm sorry. Sorry to yell at you after tonight. But—"

He stopped her then with a brusque "OK."

He waited outside while she went into her house, emerging periodically with suitcases and satchels of clothes, towels, and, finally, her cat, which she carried into her own car. He followed her Mercedes back to his house, and went straight out to the ruined shed to take up his tasks once more. He heard Nancy walking through the house, saw her move from car to door and back again carrying things. Then she came out to help him as he tore apart the remains of the roof. She had a cup of tea for him in her hands, which he took and drank, slowly, the two of them staring cautiously at each other.

Late that night—late the next morning, really—Nancy returned to her mattress on the floor of Helen's room. It was Will who ended their spat about three hours later when he got up to pee and saw her light on, knocked, then peeked around the door to find her huddled under the covers, sitting up, staring into space, the cat in her lap. She didn't want to bother him, she said to his prodding.

He sat down slowly alongside the mattress. His stomach, knees and thighs still ached from Dave's beating. He sat quietly while she talked to the wall in front of her, lapsed into silence, then started to cry. He stood up, took the cat from her lap, and pulled her up. She was wearing a long t-shirt that came to just below her knees, and socks on her feet. It was his turn to support her, one arm around her back, a hand under her shoulder as he moved her awkwardly, but insistently, along the hall, settled her into his bed, brushed a bit of her hair against the pillow cases on the two down pillows that sat there beside his own, unused. These were once Edie's; even in his lassitude, Will still changed the cases on both pillows every two weeks when he remade his bed, still puffed them up, still stuck one hand between them at night sometimes when he slept, as if there were someone there to feel his touch.

Tonight, while he himself got into the bed beside Nancy, still quietly crying, still sitting up, her arms tight about her raised knees, Will thought of Edie, and their years huddled alongside each other night after night. There were long stretches, especially in their first years together, when no bed seemed big enough, when the touch of a hand or heel made Will feel he wanted to leave town. That they survived that squeamishness, that he felt with time how treasured were her hands resting by his, were his hands on her back, along her thigh, settling for hours on her stomach: these were miracles that occupied him minutes on end during the months he was preparing himself for her death. If Will could have preserved one bit of Edie's flesh as a souvenir, it would have been the soft cavity below her neck, just below the shoulder bones and above her breasts, where he massaged her again and again during her treatments. But what was preserved instead was her laughing insistences: that he remove his watch if he wanted to hold her; that he turn over on his side so she could spoon him from behind; that they switch sides of the bed every October "so we'll get to know our asymmetries," as she put it.

Since Will's watch was already, from habit, on his bedside table, there was nothing to remove with Nancy, save the deep ache he had been living with for so long. His hands along Nancy's arm as she huddled there beside him brushed the edge of her breasts. As he awkwardly put his arms around her to see if he could quiet her hurt, one hand moved softly and slowly down her hair, stopped at her neck, rubbed its way horizontally along her shoulder line. Slowly, she rested, or acceded to Will's encouraging pressure, and slid herself down along the mattress, inside the blanket and sheet. Will felt her convolutions slow, settle. He rubbed his palm down her arm and up again, then down along hip and upper thigh, and back to her arm.

Will felt like his hand could hear her muscles quiet at his touch, though perhaps, he said to himself, the alterations he sensed were really just the result of the exhaustion that finally saves us, as he himself knew, from sobbing forever. Tired as she looked, haggard as her face seemed at times during the hours they spent cleaning the house and traveling back and forth to hers, he thought her a little less tense, less defeated perhaps, than when he put her to bed twenty-four hours earlier. He pushed himself up on an elbow and kissed her hair. When she started to cry again at that gesture, he pulled back, embarrassed and ashamed of his intrusion. At which she pulled his hand to her at the same time as she curled away from him, offering him her back while she hugged his arm tight against her. He felt the soft cloth of the t-shirt, finding a (safe, he told himself) spot along her stomach. He remembered apologizing to Edie during the next half hour while he lay there, awake. Once, he must have mumbled his thoughts aloud, because Nancy turned her face around to look at him questioningly, letting him know she too was still awake alongside him, lost in whatever thoughts possessed her. So he again lifted himself on an elbow, this time to kiss her forehead, and cheek, lightly. She smiled then, and turned her face away, into her own grief or fear or whatever it was that had brought her here. He saw her cat stretch out alongside her legs, then curl into a ball.

And that was how they got used to sleeping, and slept, the five weeks they spent alone together, and the one after that, with Helen in the house: he more soundly than he had in months, she with some nervous muscle twitches he got used to, and a kind of bubbling or popping sound that he'd hear from her lips sometimes in the early morning. He adored her body—desired it, some outside observer would no doubt insist, with every cell of his own. But the way he felt it, felt her, was as a kind of slumbering animal who gave him warmth, took his and shattered his loneliness with her unashamed need for his affection and attention.

He relished the feel of her stomach, the hints of breast and butt that came from his haphazard tossing and turning during the night. She was insistent in her need for his hand, sometimes pulling it inside the t-shirt, tugged up by the sheets, so it spread along the soft surface of a belly just beginning to thicken. She'll grow old beautifully, he thought, as his thumb and fingers discovered the line of a scar and stitches he guessed—he never asked—must have come from the twins' birth (it so resembled Edie's, though firm where hers had gone soft).

Nancy often held his hand to her through the time it took her to fall asleep—time that allowed him to settle into himself, first aroused, then quieted. When he turned to sleep himself, his hand remained, a kind of lighthouse, sentinel—he didn't have a metaphor. At times he'd wake in the night, find himself jolted by her jumpy muscles, nerves, twitches. Sometimes there were tiny peeps that came out of her, like a dreaming kitten, or, like a dog, her feet would make small running motions against his legs, scratching him with her nails. Some nights she'd wake and cry for a time, waking him as well. He learned to quiet her by just rubbing his hand slowly along her arm, up and down, up and down, the rhythm it seemed a gradual antidote to the pace of her nerves. He would get up to pee most nights and hear her cat's paws tapping along the wood floor or see the animal curled up at the foot of the bed on top of the covers.

•　　　•　　　•

As Will and Nancy settled into their life together, Will felt something let go in him. He was never sure just what triggered his reaction: the way she stood, walked, or bent; her voice as she asked if he wanted some tea or helped him sort through the blackened bits of a box from the shed; her hand holding his at night. Maybe it was how her face lifted sometimes just to look at him, curiously, or wonderingly, or merely in surprise, as she sat with a magazine or, pencil in hand, worked on one of her crossword puzzles.

Or maybe it was listening to Nancy slowly filter through her life, the details coming less as a confession than a series of leaks, like a nail-pierced tire, in small portions over a meal, while she would pet her cat or try to stack Will's rocks into mounds by shape and size, as she often liked to do. Will felt like she was doing some spring cleaning, finding this or that shirt or towel or bit of memory ready for recycling.

He watched her over the next two weeks unravel more and more of her marriage, examine parts of it she clearly hadn't looked at for a long time, and put them away in some new mound by size, shape, and importance. And mixed in were comments on what Will soon learned were the last two years: a story of Nancy and a Ken, sympathetic listener, consummate liar. That was Will's conclusion, anyway, as Nancy reported on her pleasure, her passion, her discoveries of other women the man was seeing while he promised his devotions. On and off and on again, their intimacies interrupted as often as consummated. Two-year heartsong of pain, Will decided, his housemate's quiet days suddenly interrupted by a comment, a stare off into space or tightening of her lips as a sad comprehension took her back in time.

Nancy's story was as familiar to Will as a bad movie: she met her Ken at a paralegal conference, they exchanged emails, decided to meet again, slept together, fought, slept together, fought. There was an incident with a pile of laundry on his dresser that Nancy lifted up to uncover the photograph of another woman. His mother's death brought her back to him. There were months of phone calls and emails, of pretend visits to her mother in San Francisco so she could see him; months of secrets and lying to Dave. They separated for weeks at a time, then one or the other would start things again with an email that pretended curiosity, couched desire. The cycle was repeated three or four times from what Will could make out, before some ugly encounter finally ended things.

"Late March," Nancy said, when Will asked. She seemed surprised herself discovering how recently.

And then, just minutes later, she screamed:

"On the kitchen table, for God sakes! A great fuck on the kitchen table! Then out the door! Muffins sitting in my face," Nancy said to the ceiling, while Will overheard from his position at his easel. "My muffins. The ones I bought him at that shithole bakery he loved."

Two years they were together, or sort of together, Will thought to himself. A congressman's term in office. Half a world war. The whole episode shorter than Edie's illness. Less time than some painters spend on a single canvas. Or enough time for others to complete thirty or forty, he immediately added, smiling.

May 19.

Pathetic, sad. Started to write embarrassing but why embarrassing? Just wanting—wanting someone, notice, more. Fumbling along. Reaching, getting your hand slapped, winding up holding shit.

Rocks don't seem to want that way, want that attention. Or don't let on if they do, though I pretend they whisper. Why else keep shifting

*arrangements looking for the right one except to
answer them back? Maybe that's the deception,
N's and mine: that "right" one, as if there's a
right, a one.*

Nancy's story reminded Will of high school romances: the teasing and flirting, kisses and hand squeezes he witnessed for decades in stolen moments between classes. Except, Will insisted to himself, except that these two had their own histories, more years around the hips, that (he felt) taught neither of them anything. But that's what Edie liked to say, when she heard gossip about one teacher or another starting up something, or he tartly commented on someone they knew repeating the same mistakes over and over: "Remember that the past, Mr. History, is less a lesson than a riverbed waiting for the next rain. Even yours."

Her instructions never convinced him, though her lesson was most palatable when he could respond asking why, then, he himself didn't pack it in and look for new adventure.

"Laziness, I suspect," she loved to answer. And when he would laugh, as he always did, she'd follow with the call and response that became one of their rituals:

"Remember Will, we fall in love again and again so we can tell someone our story."

"And us?" he would ask.

"We found someone who keeps listening. Despite the repetition."

At which it was his role to cross the room, whatever room they were standing or sitting in, and give her a hug. From behind when possible, while she held his hands around her from the front.

Listening to Nancy, Will started wondering at his own luck. He'd spent so little time in that loop of come and go, yes and no, in love and out. There had been Elayne, Marianne, a couple others whose names were lost to him. Marianne at least had been around enough months to make him wonder if this was what "serious" meant. But it all seemed so distant now, a kind of preschool.

As he listened to Nancy, Will kept returning in disbelief to the woman he had created watching her at night, the one he saw from the park, through the window—settled, contemplative, stable, comfortable. It was not that Nancy, but a stranger whom Will was living with: a woman who'd had a childhood driving up and down the California coast with two hippie parents, got pregnant by a local photographer of minor fame she met posing for clothes ads. ("He was in his late twenties and promised to get a divorce, but of course didn't. I modeled socks and blouses mostly.") There was a brief marriage. ("He was good to the boys but he wasn't good to me— three years of him screwing around, slamming doors and sometimes me into them.") More men, more years raising the boys alone. Then Dave, successful lawyer, who took her from her dead-end job at Kinko's to his office, retraining her as a paralegal. Son Jeff was living in Austin now with Nancy's father, who worked as a carpenter and sometime sound man, and remained still an unregenerate hippie. ("He rents a little house down there, lots of guitars around, lots of young women drifting in and out of his life.") Mom was just as unprosperous, maybe just as happy from what Will could tell. ("She's up in San Francisco, sells crystals to tourists.")

As Will caught these glimpses of Nancy's past, he felt ashamed at how interested he became—in the agonies, the self-doubt, the accusations, the anger. There was her pair of boxers with footballs and insignias of the 49ers all over them in bright orange that Nancy discovered among her stuff and threw away, explaining how Dave brought them back to her from a game last winter and asked her to wear them. And smarmy details of sex—the night, for example, when Will was cleaning his brushes and Nancy suddenly challenged him:

"Do we ever come again and again after the first few times? Have you, Will?" her face already turned back to her puzzles by the time he, blushing, was able to look at her.

Listening to Nancy's stories, and her outbursts, Will found himself insistently flipping through a Rolodex of unanswerable questions. Was it chance, the whims of time, our own distorted habits, Will wondered, that made us enter one story, find another boring? Why his fascination, after his months of denial, with Nancy's pleasures, her starts and stops, insistences and resistances? But maybe that same desire that left her bereft was her lifeline too—a pull of need and passion that led her back again and again to Ken and to Dave.

How many repetitions do we need to memorize our lessons, Will wondered, to feel linked? He thought of those old tin can and string phones: the string so short you could have talked to the other person just by lifting your voice, long enough to let you whisper so you knew it was really the string that was carrying the message. Tender in a way; silly in another. Not quite love, Will caught himself thinking; but not quite not, another part of his brain insisted. Maybe what love was for some people. Maybe something he'd missed, rather than never needed—this feeling that someone else was there at the other end of the string, however precariously, distantly, impatiently.

Will asked few questions of Nancy as she did her sifting, came out with her odd, surprising comments, or talked to him in spurts. He was mostly just happy to have her in the house, happy to hear the sound of her feet banging along the floor or the way she would click her pencil against her teeth while she sat with her crossword puzzles. And he was startled by his delight at this intrusion, when he'd spent so much energy protecting his privacy.

He heard very little about what Nancy had done with—or to—Dave after the attack. She spent many hours those first days out, told Will she was seeing people and making arrangements. Then one evening after dinner, while they were cleaning dishes, she said to him, "You don't need to worry about Dave anymore."

He nodded, waiting to hear more. But she didn't say anything until he, reluctantly, defensively, asked how she felt so sure.

She looked proud then, like a child bringing home a good grade on a test, as she explained talking to one of his partners. She and Dave signed an agreement: a promise of quiet on her part, uncontested divorce on his, some kind of rehab to try to control his drinking and temper. The document secure in a safe.

All efficiently handled, Will thought, as if Nancy were doing paralegal work on someone else's behalf, rather than to save her own life. Or, a part of him skeptically challenged, as if she'd finally gotten the leverage she needed to get out of her marriage.

For his part, Will didn't want to know more, and Nancy never brought the subject up again.

•   •   •

Without a word, Nancy accepted the odd contents of Will's house and life: the piles of driftwood, rocks, and rescued garbage, the rebuilt easel and sheet-covered table, the lack of furnishings. She did her best to create some order, but otherwise left Will alone, and didn't ask questions. Will realized that, however temporarily, or randomly, he'd found a companion he could live with. She seemed so adaptive that he soon forgot she was around for hours at a time as he again took up his struggles with paintbrush and rocks, colors and broken bottles, despite feeling it was all hopeless.

Nancy did alter some of Will's habits. His nightly walks started earlier than before, around ten p.m. They went out together, and whatever the route it always included a stop at a grocery store for the next day's food and Nancy's wine when needed. These filled Will's backpack, leaving little room for other souvenirs. They walked faster—Nancy insisted on it—and stopped less often, only when he needed to rest, until he realized the walks were less for curiosity and more for exercise. There was no dipping into garbage cans, no carrying home rocks: walking and walking, mile after mile, ending with tea for him, wine for her; an art book in his hand, a crossword puzzle or magazine or book in hers for an hour or two before cleaning the dishes and heading to bed.

Nancy's comments prompted Will to talk—mostly about Edie, mostly at night in bed, while he and Nancy held hands, before they settled into sleep. His confessions, like Nancy's, came in bits and pieces, incidents revealing and mundane from his married life popping into his head, then out his mouth before he thought much about why or who was listening. He talked especially about Edie's last months, when she was sickest. He didn't know he remembered so much, or had thought about so much.

"If I wasn't asleep on the couch, and got myself to bed, I'd wake up to go pee or just turn over and I'd see her eyes open. I know she slept. So many years beside her taught me something about her breathing that was as exact as a seismograph. I came to believe that she slept with her eyes open."

"You never asked?"

"No. I didn't want her thinking, wondering, about what she did. Whatever was happening, it seemed to me, needed to, so I left it alone."

"Just looked?"

"Looked." Will paused, listening to himself.

"I had so little to look forward to, so little time left. But what I wanted to tell you was about her eyes. I'd prop myself on my elbow and look at her, trying to take something in I could hang onto when she'd gone. Like a coffee stain in a sponge. And I'd see her staring at the shadows in the corner. I think she was looking at the flowers that were there, that I used to bring home from the farmer's market for her every week. We'd do that together, walk downtown to the market, for years, every Wednesday. When she got too tired, too frail for the walk, she made me

go. I didn't know what to pick, how to arrange flowers. I'd
carry a vase of them into the bedroom and she'd fuss, tell
me to cut this stem shorter, another at more of a diagonal,
point with her head until I got the vase where she wanted
it. During the day I'd peek in on her and find her looking
in the direction of the flowers, as if sucking light from
them, like they cast a spell. When I'd wake at night, and
look at her with her eyes open, I'd usually think that's what
she was looking at. Asleep or awake or whatever she was, I
imagined that she was staring at those shadows and shapes
of iris and lilac, rose and morning glory, that inhabited the
dark corner of the bedroom.

"I kept wondering why. Were the flowers the last thing
she saw at night? Was her face pulled in that direction by
some hypnotic dream? I don't know. Sometimes I decided
it was just a chance angle of her head where it hit the pillow
that set her sight in that direction. But whatever it was,
there were her eyes. They looked tired, day and night tired.
Not empty, not vacant. Just worn, like some sheet you'd
used for years and years. But it seemed to me there also was
something happening behind them. In slow motion, like a
replay of something from long before, a long time ago."

"You never asked about that either?"

"That?"

"The replays? If she remembered dreams she was
having? If she was reliving a special event or something?"

"No. I didn't want some history out of her. She more
and more gave up on talking, or couldn't, those last weeks, I
told you that. Like when we would sit and look through old
photos. She tried for the hundredth time in her life to sort
through the boxes and boxes of photos and label them with

names of people and dates and the rest, preparing things for Helen or me or the grandkids or whoever it was she imagined inheriting her stories. We bought a few albums and stuck the photos inside, put together a few boxes with dividers for years, sub-dividers for trips or events.

"I remember once she said to me, 'Time's a terrible fact, isn't it? You must have thought about that a lot teaching history. It seems so helpful sometimes, like canisters in the refrigerator where you put things so you can keep them in order and find them later. But once you put something away, you can never quite take it out again, can you?'

"That was when she was tiring, near the time she gave up the sorting. The last weeks, I'd just bring out the big storage boxes from the shed and put them in the bedroom one at a time. She stopped trying to explain who was in the photo or when it was taken. She would just hold one after another in her hand, sometimes only a moment, sometimes longer, then let it drop onto the blanket. Then that got to be too much and I'd just lift one or another up for her to see. She'd nod when she was done, and I'd put that photo aside and pick up the next. So maybe what she was looking at those nights was some photo she still saw in the dark. But I somehow don't think so."

"What did you imagine?"

"I tried not to. When I let myself, I had a picture of a long corridor or room. Like a hallway, where the first part was crowded with things from when she was alive all over the walls, on top of furniture and even underfoot with no chronology to them, just heaps and heaps. And as she went down the hallway there were fewer people and things on the walls and floor. Everything got more barren. But not barren exactly—just less and less stuffed with the life, more and more with some other kind of substance."

"Your idea of heaven."

"Of something else. I'm not a heaven type. Just something else, just not life."

"Or rocks."

He looked at her then, next to him. Turned his head away, staring instead at the ceiling.

"Or rocks. You're right to say that. I do think they're closer. Yes. To what's not the melodrama."

"And us? Here together in bed like this? Are we the melodrama?"

"Oh my yes! What else could we be but afternoon soap opera?"

At which they both smiled, and she moved her face close to his and let her lips sit on his, mouths closed, for a long moment before pulling away to fall back onto her own pillow. Neither said anything else that night, though he reached his hand out across her thigh, found hers atop her stomach, wound his fingers into hers and pulled the arm down along her side. It wasn't long before he felt the fingers of her hand relax, only a little longer before his too grew slack in sleep.

•   •   •

She left him—he felt it as desertion, despite the way his brain insisted this wasn't the case; she wasn't leaving, he had no claims—for three nights with her mother in San Francisco. He wondered, of course, if the time also included Ken, but decided, despite his jealous pangs, that it didn't, but was instead one long series of phone calls to everyone who might have heard from or seen Jess. Will was left with Scotty the cat, whom he tended with indifferent attention, though he appreciated the weight of the animal at the foot of the bed mornings as he woke, watching it stretch itself and arch onto its legs before offering Will a polite hungry whimper.

It was Will who finally got a note from Jess while Nancy was gone. It was a small envelope with the return address of a motel, the Oilman's Inn, on the upper corner. The stamp said the message was mailed from Bakersfield, CA, two days earlier. Inside the envelope Will found a strip of photos from the kinds of booths you found at amusement parks or bus stations, showing the boy's face, unshaven but smiling, hair a little mussed as if maybe he'd just awakened, holding up the edge of one of Will's paintings. On the back, in a tiny script Will could barely make out, Jess had written:

> OK so far. Heading south & east. Your
> paintings grow on me. They're nice company.
> Please call Mom and let her know I'm OK. I
> told her to come see you if she needs to. I hope
> you'll help her. Sorry and thanks.

Will called Nancy; that likely prompted her to return earlier than she'd planned, though even after reading and rereading the note she seemed as worried about her son as before. They resumed their lives together: the painting, the magazines, the crossword puzzles, the walks and wine and tea, the nights in bed.

•   •   •

Those were quiet and quieting days for Will. He painted. Nancy moved about the house or went off on her own to appointments or to wander the town, without telling Will why or goodbye. He heard her talking with her mother on the phone, or closing the door of the washroom; stood near her as he tore lettuce for a salad while she watched over a boiling pan of pasta.

It was in this interlude—precious then, more precious still later, when Will looked back to it—that he started writing in his notebook only when Nancy was around. Sometimes it was across the kitchen counter while she sat on a stool she brought over from her house, or on the living room floor, while she sprawled out on five or six pillows she'd collected from various abandoned beds in his and her home and reassembled into a reading corner. One day, instead of talking about color or rocks, he realized he was writing to Edie.

So Edie: In the last days, when you were sleeping more than awake, or only seemed to be (I was never sure), I used to sit by your bed and tell you the story of your life. A scrap here, a note there. I never knew if you heard me, and by the second hour of talking to you I didn't much care. I knew you were dying, knew all I could do for you was sit, hold your hand, witness you moving away, and talk, until you decided or whatever it is that decides decided you could quit. Or you did whatever it was you were doing those last weeks, in dying.

It was pretty clear to me even then that I didn't know squat about what was happening to you. It was pretty clear even then that I was sitting there for me, to let me believe that anything I could say might hold you in this world a little longer.

Helen would disappear about 8 or 9 after the dishes were clean, the floor swept, the clothes folded: her way to pretend she could control the world. She would come in and give you one of those solemn kisses of hers. I was supposed to go somewhere too, she insisted, though she knew that my smile and nods were only polite and I'd do what I did, whatever she said. So I'd stay where I was, sit at the side of the bed, sometimes lie down next to you, sometimes hold your hand, pretend I felt some squeeze, and begin.

Will looked across the kitchen counter, out the back door with its patch of cardboard still covering the panes Jess broke, into the pale light, just shaping itself into dark silhouettes that defined his neighbor's fence and slanted garage rooftop. It was hard now to remember Edie well: the thickening body of her healthy years, the rounding stomach, the thighs strong from her habitual hour's walk each afternoon after school. The thinness of those last months was what he saw now: her body reduced, narrow in bed beside him, the skin soft and sagging to his touch. He bent down to his notebook.

It took three nights, the telling: three nights to say everything I could remember—all you told me, we told each other; all I held onto that we had done together. The fact that you kept breathing, and breathing and breathing, no matter how shallow and short the breaths became, made me believe that you were listening. That I wasn't too off in what I reported about something you knew better than I ever would. I guess I kept hoping you'd correct me in some detail, or remind me that your years going crazy for Bobby the one who was studying to be a circus clown came before the three months you followed Andy down to New Orleans and lived on gumbo and tourist handouts; that you didn't really hit a cop with an umbrella during the protests in Chicago in '68; or that you were in jail eight days and not five when you got arrested at Livermore. I remember that I was careful when I talked not to make up too much, not even to tell you how much I gloated over what you'd done, the bravery, the lack of clarity that somehow blessedly brought you to me.

You never stopped me, so I just kept going, down to the end, to when we found out you had cancer the first time, the operations, the chemo and radiation, the remissions, the return, the resignation, the pain. Down to the bits of time we made love and I rubbed your body down and up, back and front, relieving your aches you assured me, absolving my guilt I know, preserving in the prints of my fingers whatever I could of your skin and muscles. Up to the third night, saying goodbye. Asking you if there were anything I'd forgotten. My way to tell you it was OK to leave, move on, stop, whatever it was you did, dying. I've wondered sometimes why I didn't record the story. I realize no one really cared about the facts but me. And maybe you. And of course it wasn't the facts I cared about at all, it was you. Slow learner, this historian.

Will smiled. Historian. "History teacher," he would insist, when anyone at a party would ask him what he thought about time, history, the idea of progress. "I'm no historian," he'd explain, in a quip he refined and repeated year after year. "I'm like someone force-feeding ducks and geese, stuffing adolescents with the unbelievable notion that the world existed before they were born." He'd smirk at his own cynicism, an alias hiding the passionate hope he carried into every class that he could help his students learn not to trust what they were told about who they were and where they came from. What was all that, he wondered now, twirling his ballpoint, staring at the label like he hadn't ever noticed it before. What was I hiding, protecting, ashamed of?

Here I am, Edie, back at the wheel, lost, waiting for you to help me navigate the way you used to when we'd drive somewhere, my sense of direction fractured as a broken foot. I've been spending my days looking at rocks and bottles and vases. The rocks are good to me. They're patient. They don't criticize. I can fail and for the first time in years and years not feel like I'm paying for my awkwardness. It seemed like the right thing to do, this painting. I thought you'd understand. I remember thinking that when I started moving the furniture out, and again when I got going on the wall: you'd hate living in this, but you'd laugh if it were someone else's life or story.

And it was: it was mine, without you. And I got better, I think. Or a little better, anyway. Not better like a doctor talks about, or better at painting—I'll always be shit with a brush in my hand, as inept at this as I used to be when you made me refinish chairs with you. But I thought I could see better, know what made a shape interesting, look and not stop paying attention. That stuff started to matter. It made more sense than anything else. It made me think of you and your pleasure looking at paintings. I remember thinking that I'd left out museums when I retold you who you were. I hadn't the faintest idea what to say about all your hours walking those crowded rooms, all the late evenings you spent with catalogues in your lap, all those times we'd push aside some tome you'd left on the bed in the midst of starting to make love or I'd feel one beneath a foot as I adjusted myself with you. I didn't know what to say.

Remember how you used to laugh at me these last years, sitting beside the bed, holding your hand, as I picked up one art book after another? And here I am these last months, staring at these books, wondering what I'd missed. Sometimes by your bedside I'd get stuck on one painting for a couple minutes, you staring at me staring at the book in my lap. "Where are you?" you'd ask me, and I'd turn the book to you, offering whatever page was open as if offering you some foreign world. But now I think it wasn't what the painting showed that I got stuck on but something smaller: some odd bit of color out of place, a brushstroke, the dark entrance to some house along a road. A distraction, a hit of something curious enough to pull at my attention,

*take me out of my own whirl, my brain, my
worries. I just got, thankfully, stuck—stuck on
something that let me not be stuck on what I knew
was coming: no more you. That's what I want from
the rocks too, I think, as much as I want anything I
can name. To get stuck. To find something that
keeps me staring. They seem so solid, Edie, so not
me, so themselves. They just sit there. No doctor's
appointments, no plans for vacations, no gifts to
buy for Christmas. You can get stuck on anything,
and when you get stuck, you're stuck. And
everything answers back, in its way.*

*I just wanted time to sit. That's what I told
myself when I started. Part of me does, I think,
still. But I couldn't stay in place, like my still
lifes. I kept looking for something. On my walks,
my garbage raids, my keyhole nights looking in
on strangers. I'm lost the way I get lost, with
people. In the human crap again. I don't want to
be that person anymore, I claim. Then there I
am. So I guess I do. Or am. I don't know what to
call it. But I can't pretend it's not me, can I?*

*I was pretty happy. Maybe happy isn't the word,
since everyone is happy or trying hard to be these
days. That's not what I felt. But I took care of
myself, in my way. I was interested, and you're the
one who knows how that's not always my state of
mind. Then the invasions began: Kitty, Benny.
Then Jess, now Nancy and that lover of hers and
her husband. They've clogged up the plumbing. It's*

like all the vases and rocks are wearing masks now, little faces chattering away, asking me when I'll be done so I can come help, expecting me to do something to make things better. I don't know how to make things better. I never did, for you or me or even my students, I guess.

He knew that wasn't so, couldn't be true. He helped Edie, he knew, letting her let him into her life. Helped her be happy again. Helped Helen grow up. Helped make the days pass. Helped Edie through her last years. He could give himself a little credit, at least, by now. But he let the line sit there, a comforting accusation.

For a little while I knew how to look at a rock and not have my attention waver. I knew what it meant to wonder what colors had to do with each other. I saw this town in the night when it was all darkness, absence, silence, dreams. I could be by myself and not miss anyone. No one. No one, sometimes not even you. I didn't get angry anymore, didn't swear, didn't throw things, didn't, well ... didn't bother anyone. For you that was never enough, not to be a nuisance, you always tried to make things better. But for me, that was enough, is enough I think, because I still don't get what better can be, for any of these people, let alone me. What's better about Benny living with his loony grandmother instead of his wacko parents? Or me, in our bed with Nancy beside me and her cat prowling the house? Is that any better than rocks, paint on my hands and on the floor?

Maybe better isn't it either. Maybe it's all maybe, though when I write a line like that I can see you giving me that look of yours at my way of complicating things. And your goddamned aphorism, like life was a political slogan: "Being afraid of being wrong can't ever be right."

Right. Not helpful, sweetheart, but right. As always.

•   •   •

Kitty called three weeks after the fire. Nancy answered and passed the phone to Will. He was standing at his easel, though he quickly moved off and out of the room.

"You've got visitors."

"Yes."

"Who answer your phone."

"Yes. Anxious about her son."

"And you've had some excitement, I hear."

"Who's your source?"

"Roger, the garden hunk. He reads, you know."

"I expected he did. But maybe not the local newspaper. Or not to notice articles about your friends."

"He notices a lot more than the aphids on the lemon tree. Who is she?"

"Her name's Nancy."

"That doesn't tell me much."

"It's complicated."

"I've got time."

"Not now."

"Sometime?"

"Yes, but not now."

"Because there's something you don't want to tell me?"

"Because I don't know what to say yet."

"Preplanning. From the man trying to just react to rocks. You are still doing the rocks thing?"

"Yes, still at the rocks. No, not preplanning. I just don't know what's happening, I can't say."

"Or don't want to, to me."

"Or don't want to, to you. Or however you want to think about it. It's not about you, or me either."

"But about someone else."

He sighed, trying to think of a way through the conversation.

"Yes, a couple someone elses. It's not done yet."

"For the someone elses or for you? Or are you one of the someone elses?"

"For them. And for me too. Can we stop this?"

"No preliminary progress reports? Speculations about the future? Prognostications for the stockholders? No, we can't, not yet."

"Good to know you have an investment."

"You've always known that, Will, even when you didn't want to."

Will realized he had nothing to say to that, and didn't. It took a moment for Kitty to fill in the silence.

"How about you? Can you talk about you? How are you, are you involved, hurt?"

"Was hurt, now fine. Still painting. Not sure what involved means."

"Something happened at the house that night that didn't get into the newspapers, right?"

"Right."

"And there was a fire."

"Right. No more shed."

"And no more what was in the shed."

"Right."

"That's all right with you?"

"Seems to be. Yes."

"All the photos? The keepsakes?"

"Gone."

"No regrets about that?"

"No. Nothing's missing I need."

That stopped her for a moment.

"I'll let that one go for now. It was messier than the newspapers reported, and it landed someone—the she-person who answered the phone—in your house, right?"

"Right."

"For how long?"

"I'm not sure."

"Days?"

"Or weeks. I'm not sure. What's with you? With Samantha and Benny and Benny's dad, what's his name?"

"Evan. I'm stringing along a state or two away doing my own exploring, waiting for the next report."

"Me too," Will said, grasping at this straw.

"Sounds like you're a bit closer to the action."

"Yes and no."

At which Kitty paused, quiet on her end, until she realized Will would not go on.

"OK."

"OK?"

"Shit no, not OK. But OK for now. Best I can get from you, it sounds like."

Will took a little satisfaction in that.

"When will I see you again?"

"I'm not sure. I'll check in soon though."

"I'd like that."

"Really?"

"Of course."

"Really?"

"Yes."

"Not yes and no?"

"No. Yes."

He heard her laugh, take in some breath, waiting for more.

"Yes and no. But don't disappear."

"I never have, for long."

   •   •   •

It was the night after Will's talk with Kitty that Will suddenly stopped his writing in mid-sentence and looked up at Nancy, engrossed in her crossword puzzle. Sensing Will's shift in attention, Nancy lifted her head and looked at him.

"You don't think much of my paintings," he asked.

She looked around her, up and down the walls, as if trying to give them a second chance.

"I guess not. I mean I don't dislike them, or the other stuff around the house—the rocks and wood and all. I don't know what you're up to and I suppose I don't really care."

After a pause, perhaps thinking that what she had said might feel dismissive, or just to be clearer, she added, "What I mean is, I don't think much about your paintings, or about anything else around here, one way or another. It's what you're doing."

Nancy paused, as if still uncertain what she wanted to convey.

"I'm not getting this right," she continued. "It's your house. It's comfortable for me. I'm fine that you're doing what you're doing. It seems to make you happy."

Again she stopped, smiled.

"Or at least not unhappy."

Will nodded, and realized he would have to be content with that. He was, in fact, surprised that he wasn't. What did he want from Nancy? he asked himself. Admiration? A chance to be her teacher again? Questions about this world of rocks and paint where he knew he was as dense as could be? Writing about his reactions only made the confusion more obvious to him.

Maybe it was this confusion, maybe something else, that made Will offer Nancy his notebooks two nights later. The two of them were again sitting across from each other at the counter: him writing, her working on her crossword puzzles. Will got up, went to his bedroom, and came back with three more notepads. He handed these, and the pad he had been writing in, across the kitchen counter to Nancy. Each was dated, creating a sequence of books covering the months since the previous July. She put down her pencil, looked at the covers, glanced back at Will. Asking a question, Will felt. He saw a "What?" or "Why?" or just perhaps a "Huh?" sitting in her pupils.

"My notebooks," he explained, realizing in all their days and nights together he'd never said anything to her about what he was writing, and that she'd never asked.

She looked down, located the earliest one, and started shuffling through the first pages. Standing across the kitchen counter from her, Will saw his uneven handwriting that ignored the lines on the paper, that covered the pages from margin to margin with barely a space between paragraphs, that to his eye, or memory, displayed his feverish energy.

Will felt himself blush. Somehow Nancy sensed that too, looked up at him again, and even reached her hand across to rest it on his arm, just below the elbow, maybe to reassure him, or thank him for this odd gift.

"You don't have to read them," he told her. "Or certainly not all of them. But I need to let you. Seems time. Seems fair, after my hours in the trees, looking at you."

She smiled at him then, and rubbed the side of his face, scratchy as always from the haphazard way he shaved.

"There's no fair, Will. Ever, I'm getting to think. But thank you, I think."

She smiled then, looking down at the work ahead of her.

"You're not paying back a debt here. But I will read them, if you want me to."

That was a question that required more from Will than he was ready for.

Eventually he nodded, said, "Yes, I think I want you to," and left her there at the counter with the pads in her hands, while he went to the living room to paint.

That didn't work. After spending almost an hour watching her as she moved from counter to pillows back to counter again, he went for a walk, the first one he'd taken alone for weeks. How long was it, he asked himself, wandering along paths that had become unfamiliar to him. Just over three weeks, he realized, smiling.

Will could picture her reading, slowly, the way she did (he still liked to imagine) those long nights when he watched from the park—sometimes pausing to stare out to space, sometimes moving on, sometimes holding a page open for long periods, sometimes skimming. Stopping to sip some wine, rub her cat, stare through him, invisible in the darkness of the trees, staring back at her.

When he came home Nancy handed the pads back to him. She smiled, hugged him to her (his arms helplessly flat against his sides). "Thank you," she said.

He felt her waiting for a cue from him to help her see what to say next. He said nothing, though, leaving her on her own.

She started by laughing, which made him pull back a bit from her hand, still holding onto his left arm.

"No, don't pull away, you. I'm laughing because I don't really know what to say. I kept thinking about you looking at me, all those nights. I realized how little you knew about me then, or even do now. You understand?"

I do, he thought, but again didn't answer or even nod his head.

"We don't show as much of ourselves as we think we do, even here, in this stuff you've written, do we?"

He didn't react, waiting for something more.

"Most of this is so … technical, I guess the word is. Or detailed about things I hadn't noticed. All that stuff about each rock and space and light. You do go off, you know. About things I don't ever think about. Made me want to keep my eyes open more, I guess."

Then she looked down for a moment, letting one hand stray across the top notepad.

"You're confusing," she told him. "You must know that. Or haven't you ever reread these yourself?"

"Never," he admitted.

"Of course not," she said with a laugh. "I should have known. You've been too busy."

She smiled at him then, took his face in both hands, making a "V" under his chin, and pushed up on her tiptoes to kiss him, lightly, on the forehead, then the tip of the nose, then lips.

And that was all that either said then. Or for the next two days—Will afraid to ask and Nancy not talking, while they exchanged comments about food, the cold night air, and the new shingles they saw on a house they passed. It was just before bed that second night that Nancy said to him:

"Will, it's good that you wrote all that. It must have helped, I guess. I don't understand a lot of it. It doesn't make sense, to me at least. But that's OK, you know. Or ought to know by now. Same way your house is OK, and your paintings are OK, and you are OK. More than OK, with your slumped shoulders and mussy hair and your clothes with paint all over them."

Will had always been a bit vain about his posture, so he took in her remarks with a little less pleasure than he might have otherwise. But Nancy wasn't quite done.

"Heartbreak takes lifetimes to heal, doesn't it? Slower than a broken toenail, that's for sure."

He nodded, not sure where she was going with all this.

She paused, looked up at the ceiling.

"When I was raising the boys, after my marriage, drifting from one asshole to another, I was so lonely, and so afraid of the bed and the dark and being there just by myself, that I would sleep with all the lights on. I'd read all these books—the ones that tell you how to make your life better. One after another, mostly standing there in a bookstore, leafing through them, because I couldn't afford to buy them. I'd write down lines that seemed wise, and then put them by the bed for when I woke up at night. 'Tears don't leave scars; they're why Kleenex was invented.' I remember that one. And, 'It's normal to be sad when you lose a dream'—that made me feel like there was some good reason for what I was going through.

"But the one I'd keep going back to was from Khalil Gibran."

Will felt himself scowl when he heard Gibran's name—partly because he himself had done his time reading those little books; partly because he couldn't remember a wedding or funeral he'd ever been to that didn't have some maudlin quote that someone carted out, as if offering a taste of God's wisdom.

Nancy didn't seem to notice his reaction.

"Gibran said something about how if you keep your heart open, your pain is as good and fulfilling as your happiness. Something like that. Whatever it was, that's what I remember. And I still try to remember that. And I thought of that reading your notebooks."

Will nodded, like he understood what she was saying. But her reaction was meaningless to him, except to make him wonder, again, just what he expected of her, of anyone—even himself.

But she wasn't done.

"I don't think I get you any more now than I did before. Before I read the notebooks, I mean. Oh, I do, some things. Like you and Edie. But I never doubted that you two loved each other. So I'm not sure you make more sense to me than you did before you gave me the books. And the fact that I don't get you doesn't really matter to me. What really matters is that you were around when you were around, even if I didn't want you to be. Jess was right: you could help me. And you did. And here we are."

That also wasn't what Will expected to hear. And though later, weeks later, thinking back to his reactions, he realized how kindly Nancy had served him, at that moment Will was hurt. He remained hurt even when she hugged him, kissed both cheeks, and ran her hands through his hair. She must have felt his distance, because she didn't reach out for him that night or the one after that, but waited until he reached for her, his hand asking to return to its place spread out over her stomach, where she covered it with hers, tightly, warmly, firmly, through the night.

6

IT ALSO WAS NANCY WHO ANSWERED Helen's phone
call. Will was used to Nancy rushing to the phone every
time it rang, hoping she might hear from Jess. He had
gotten used to most of Nancy's habits in the four weeks
she'd been in the house: her way of picking up dishes from
the counter before he was through with them; her bright
red bras and silk blouses and jeans, her way of licking the
wood on pencils when she sat each night with the three
papers she insisted on walking downtown to buy, and read
cover to cover, before she settled down with one crossword
puzzle after another, for up to two hours most days.

When Nancy handed Will the phone, he was greeted
by Helen's anxiety voice.

"Who was that?"

"Nancy. A friend."

"What's she doing there at midnight?"

"Living here."

"With you? Just the two of you?"

"Yes and no. And her cat. She's looking for her son."

"At your house at midnight?"

"No. It's a long story. Why are you calling me at midnight?"

"Are you shacking up with her, Dad?"

"Not the way you're asking. She's here to get away from her husband, who was beating her."

"Not to look for her son?"

"That too."

He realized he was hearing a lot of noise around Helen.

"Where are you?"

"At the San Jose airport. What's she doing at the house?"

Will realized Helen wasn't going to quit without more explanation. But he'd had enough of listening to himself try to explain. He glanced at Nancy, nestled in her corner of the living room, book and wine glass alongside, dressed in the same drab gray sweatshirt and baggy pants he'd been admiring on her since he first spied her through her window.

"What are you doing at the airport?"

"I flew in to see you. I was worried about you. Now I'm more worried."

"Don't be. Why didn't you let me know?"

That shifted the discomfort to Helen, who (he could only guess, knowing her overlarge conscience) was right now struggling with her desire to accuse him of something—she still didn't quite know what, but something having to do with his lax indifference to her and her kids and everyone else these last months. And what must have looked to her like some scandal he was getting himself into. And her own embarrassment at taking this way to find out about him, by surprising him, late at night, with a forty-five-minute warning that she'd be parking in the driveway. And staying a week or so, she said, vaguely, as if time wasn't something to worry about.

Will watched Nancy while he talked: sitting on her pile of pillows, surrounded by some broken pieces of wood from the table and the crisscrossed diagrams that still covered the wood floor. She looked comfortable scrunched over her crosswords, which rested inches from her face against her raised knees, her hair half covering her face, unconsciously tapping the metal surrounding the eraser against her bottom teeth.

This was not a sight Helen would admire, though his own pleasure increased from hour to hour, day to day.

A breath of life was the phrase he used in his notebook: *Air, wind, gusts of weather after many months.*

He was still startled by how much, and how quickly, it had all dropped—that need to protect himself, his privacy, whatever it was—dropped like a piece of paper falling from his hand. The night after Dave's rampage, or the day after that, or the day after—he never was quite sure when. Or why. But disappear it did, like the silk scarf in the magician's hand.

It would be hard, he thought, to explain this to Helen—to anyone, he realized, but maybe especially to Helen, who so idolized Edie. He remembered how her husband, Amos, talked to the point of weariness about how much he'd heard of Will and Edie and their marriage. No,

Helen would have some trouble with this, he was sure, which meant he was going to have trouble. Nancy too, who saw the difficulties in a moment when he said goodbye to his daughter, turned to her, and explained that Helen would be there in an hour or less, to stay for a few days.

Nancy immediately asked about arrangements: Should she go? Find another place to stay? And where should she sleep tonight?

It was the word "should" that Will wanted to point out to her, wondering idly how often it did or didn't come up in crossword puzzles, and what the clue might be ("what you say when you don't want to do what someone else thinks you ought to"). The two of us seemed to have gotten rid of the term, he thought, watching Nancy as she hastily stood up, collected her newspapers, sipped the last of the wine in her glass, and headed to the kitchen to start what he could only assume was a desperate effort to tidy things up before Helen arrived. He was not quite sure how she planned to do that, since the one thing she couldn't tidy up was her own presence in the house, his bed, and his life. But he guessed she was already trying to figure out how to deal with that issue as well.

As he watched Nancy jolting herself back into respectability, he wondered what Helen's visit might cost him, and what he was willing to pay. A long-standing gnawing was gone these last weeks. Against that, he had to balance Nancy's sensibilities—or what he could imagine they were. Could she live as they had with his daughter in the house?

Will spent the next half hour listening to Nancy ask questions he couldn't answer: Why was Helen coming, and

146

coming now? Was he happy to see her? Did she know about me? What did she know about me? Do you want me to go? Is there anything I can do?

Will had few answers: he didn't know why now, but suspected it had to do with his long silence and solitude; of course he was happy to see her, but she wasn't one for surprises like this and he wasn't quite ready for this one; she knows just what you heard me tell her on the phone; I don't want you to go; you could help me make up the bed in her room for her and maybe free up some space in her closet.

Will watched Nancy move to the back bedroom to take her own small store of clothes out of the stacked packing crates she had assembled as her dresser, grab hangers of jeans and pants, and stand in the center of the room with them in her arms. She dropped them in a heap on the still dusty rug and circled the room with her eyes, making sure she'd found every trace of herself. She grabbed a few more assorted t-shirts and tops from the makeshift shelves, picked up the hangers and rushed down the hall to Will's bedroom, where she dropped the clothes on her side of the bed. Will followed, watching as she rushed back to the washroom, trailing new variations of the same unanswerable questions behind her.

It was at the hall closet that Will finally caught up with her and firmly held her arms to her sides so she would stop reaching up for the sheets. She tensed and resisted as he tried to turn her around.

"You'll need to decide, Nancy. I'm happy with how we live, how we sleep, how we've settled in. I don't want to change that, not a thing, and don't need to for Helen's sake."

He found he had run through his speech and didn't know what came next as she looked at him. Surprised, he thought; suspicious, he was sure.

"You have to decide," he repeated, stepping back, letting her go.

She looked at him for a few moments more and nodded her head downward the tiniest bit before turning again to reach for the sheets, pull them down, check for pillow cases, ask him behind her back if these were the ones that fit the mattress in Helen's room.

To which Will offered a barked "Yes!" before he turned away and headed down the hall to the living room and his brushes and paint. He heard her behind him shut the closet, turn in the opposite direction to Helen's bedroom. Then heard her up the hall again, heard metal banging against metal, eventually heard the sound of the vacuum cleaner. How many months, he wondered, since that's been out of the closet? The rug under the mattress, of course. In the quiet after the vacuuming, he heard the soft swish of her bare feet on the rug as she moved along the sides of the mattress, heard the snap of the sheet in the air as she billowed it out over the bed. He didn't hear her again until he saw an edge of gray as she came to the door to the living room and stood there until he turned to look at her. He couldn't see his own face, but when he thought about it later, he felt ashamed for his pout, the rage and hurt and anguish that must have been hanging along the lines of his set chin, lined brow, the bags under his eyes.

"Will, Will, Will. I like you, like the way we live. So much! Let's see how it goes. It might help us both if you

washed that paint off your face and broke your jaw open
a little."

She came into the room then, moved to his
half-turned face, smiled at him and kissed his cheek. Her
hand came up to his head, pushed up the back of his hair
from the neck across to the point of his receding hairline.
Then her fingers spread, as her palm washed down over
his forehead, eyes, cheeks, mouth and chin, like a towel.
She quickly kissed him again, on the other cheek, and
then turned back to the hall and the bedding.

"Oh, and can you find somewhere to put all those
clothes of mine that I just threw onto the bed? Probably
not the best place for them."

Will put away his brushes and headed for the
bedroom. His closet was bare—or nearly so—and it
calmed his mind to sift through Nancy's clothes and
separate underwear, tops, jeans, and the rest, see some
skirts and dresses hanging alongside his unworn sports
jackets. Then he turned back to the living room to see
what kind of repairs he could make. There was little that
could be done, he decided, besides cleaning his brushes
and smoothing a tarp that sat in a heap alongside one of
the rock piles. There were a few raw wood pieces he'd
thrown down next to his bottles. He could remove them.
But where would they go that Helen wouldn't see them
anyway? He stuck the few toys that lay scattered around
into a cardboard box, looked again with anguish at what
he knew Helen would see, or miss seeing, and then just
shrugged his shoulders, went to the kitchen counter, and
opened his notebook:

*Fallen into mooning old age. Into resentments
and anger, into regret that I wasted so much
time. Wrong. Regret I didn't waste more. Helen
coming: like clocking into work again. Who's
running the company? Think you'll get fired?*

Helen was as prickly as he imagined she would be as
she came in, dropped her bag, kissed Will on the cheek
and turned, expectantly, for a glimpse of the woman he'd
called Nancy.

Nancy had changed into a blouse and slacks, and stood
behind the kitchen counter, pouring hot water into a teapot,
discreetly providing Will with whatever space he could find
between the two of them. The introductions were brief, and
quickly interrupted by Helen glancing in the other direction,
towards the living room with its covered windows,
paint-smeared floor, and piles of rocks, bottles, and pillows.

"Oh my God, Dad! What have you done! I heard it
was crazy, but this."

She walked into the room, stood at his repaired easel,
looked down on the mottled browns and greens and grays
that he was working with that day, and stared at the walls
surrounding the fireplace, filled with other pieces of
Masonite. Then she did a slow three-sixty turn.

When she looked up at her father, all he said back to
her was, "Heard from whom?"

His question stopped her. She mumbled, "Kitty. She
called a few days ago, worried."

Will didn't pursue this, but he realized that if Kitty had
called Helen, his daughter knew there was a woman in his
house long before she heard Nancy's voice on the phone.

The information, or Helen's uneasy confession of it, provided a bit of leeway for him as he maneuvered through the next few hours. Helen accepted, or acquiesced, to things. She followed Will down the hall to her old room, passing Benny's drawings, most hanging still in tatters after Dave's attacks, glanced without a word at the boxes in her closet that were not there when she left months before, accepted the mattress on the floor (it rested on the wooden bed frame from her childhood when she had left). She accepted too, it seemed, the bathroom counter with Nancy's toothbrush, hairbrush, and skin creams arranged neatly by what used to be Edie's sink. And she said nothing when the night ended, and she had to hear Nancy and her father repair to the bedroom, cross the threshold and close the door. Will felt for his daughter, and thanked her to himself (and to her, the next day, on their walk) for her stoicism, or politeness, or whatever it was that helped her endure the strange welcome home. This was not the house she left, not the house she loved, he knew that. But it was the house he could offer her, and he was willing to do that much, if not much more, for the stepdaughter he loved.

The rest of Helen's stay turned out easier than Will expected—or maybe, a part of him kept insisting, had a right to hope. There were a few difficult moments as she pressed him for details—What was he doing? (What she saw.) Did he know why? (No, except that it felt right.) How long had he been living in the house this way? (Since you left; end of the summer.) What happened to all the furniture, the silver, the commemorative plates? (Gone to charity, destroyed in the fire, broken.)

Will found himself answering her less defensively than he expected—not so much proud of his new life as aware, in the act of answering his daughter, that it was his, however odd or misshapen it might seem. He assured her that he knew his paintings were worthless, but loved what he was doing. That he was fine, or nearly so—or as fine as he had been since Edie died. That he loved her and her kids and Amos, but needed this time alone. Of course the word "alone" got him a few angry words from Helen, since he was far from alone. He laughed at her "fussiness," as he called it. He said very little, in fact, when Helen asked him directly if Nancy was now a fixture in his life, someone he cared about, loved—a new in-law or partner or whatever the current term might be.

"She quiets me," was all Will said, after a long enough pause that Helen stopped walking beside him and started to cry. He took his daughter in his arms, let her lean her head against him, and nodded his own head up and down, surprised by his clarity.

The closest Will came to knowing what he himself was thinking about or hoping came later that week, when Helen returned again, as she did every day, to the question of Will's new roommate. They were again walking slowly along a path that skirted the bay water, surrounded by others on their own missions: people running or striding purposefully by in tights or sweats, bikers passing in one direction or another, parents pushing strollers or holding a child's hand, folks walking their dogs. Drummers and loungers occupied the benches and grassy lawns that lined the pathway.

"Are you trying to save her?"

"Save her? From what? From her husband? No, thank you; he's bigger than me."

"From herself then."

"I can't imagine how I could. Even your mother it turned out couldn't save me."

"Save, help, rescue. What's the right word?"

"You pick. Her son Jess will call eventually. She'll go off to see him. She'll come back to town maybe and maybe not. I'll likely see her sometimes. If she's lucky, or the guy is lucky, she'll meet someone and fall in love and be happier than she is now."

"But not with you?"

"Oh, she's already in love with me, and me with her. That doesn't count."

"Because you aren't lovers?"

"Because we help each other."

"How? You don't seem to let anyone do that."

"No. Or yes, you're right. I don't. But they do anyway. It's happening all the time, whether I want it to or not. You're helping me by coming to town, even if I didn't want you to, and by objecting to everything I do, even if I wish you didn't. She's helping me by needing me to help her."

"And that's all? That's what this is about for the two of you?"

"No. That's not all, but it's all you'll hear from me. Or her, I suspect, if you asked her. Which I am pretty sure you won't."

"And the painting?"

"Oh, the painting. Well, sometimes I think I'm learning that color, or maybe color and shape, is enough to make life worth living. I think that even if I never get my colors the way I want them, even when I watch the shapes and shadows defeat me, again and again. I think all this helps keep me alive. And that's more than I knew a few months ago about why stay alive."

•   •   •

It was two days after that conversation when Will's prophesies about Nancy turned real. Nancy started each day with a call to her father and son Jeff in Austin, hoping that Jess might find his way there when his money ran out. And one morning it was Jess who answered. Will was just setting up his paints for the day, Helen was washing the morning's dishes. Both turned in surprise as Nancy started yelling her son's name and crying into the phone. She banged a fist hard along the kitchen wall in her surprise, pleasure, anger, or whatever group of emotions pushed her along. Will's Masonites rattled on their wires.

She called Jess back three times that day and twice the day after, though she said little to Will about her son. He was fine; he was tired; he was resting; he thought he'd stay in Austin for now and find a job. He asked about Will, she said. She told Will Jess had heard she was at Will's house from his brother, Jeff. When the time came, it was Helen who volunteered to take Nancy to the airport on Friday of that week. He felt flattened by gloom, the sadness of knowing that everything right was happening and it brought him pain. His final goodbyes to Nancy were brief.

"You know how much you matter to me," she said, rather than asked.

"Yes, and you to me," he answered as she hugged him, put her lips up to his, reached her hand out to brush his bits of beard upward across his cheeks and jaw, and smiled.

"I will be back, you know."

"But not here," he said.

"Not likely, but you never can tell. I do need to collect Scotty. Assuming she'll ever want to leave you or you'll part with her by then."

He smiled.

"Not likely she'll forget you," was all he could get out before he felt tears starting to collect at the edges of his eyes. She saw them, wiped them away, kissed him again.

"Thanks for putting up with me."

"And with me," he answered, and squeezed her arm one more time before she picked up her suitcase and headed for Helen's rented car.

Will's entry in his notebook was brief:

To give consent to passing time. All my life I dreamed I might, maybe, one day. To approve of the day ending without wishing for the end not to come. Or pleading for it to come earlier as a reprieve from anguish or guilt, boredom or fear.

And time doesn't give a shit for our consent or interest. Nancy here, Nancy gone, I stay. Helen here, soon be gone, I stay. Jess gone, was here, I stay. Until I don't.

Until seems long tonight.

And the next day, another entry, before he could turn more of his attention back to Helen and his easel:

Learning from the crap, from not getting what you
want. Until you finally give up, and look at always
like it's not only your enemy. Even if my always is
me missing Edie, missing Nancy, or whoever. But
that's also me making the missing what I have.
Until I've made a thing of it, as if it matters. Until
it does matter? Enough, today, to think so.

Helen's trip, he learned over the next two days, was not just a rescue mission. She wanted some time away from Amos and the kids—from a round of little spats that left her exhausted and lonely each night, afraid there was too little in her life. Will found himself handing out advice, listening to himself know something about marriage. The night before Helen was to leave the conversations intensified as they sat together around a pizza box and bowl of salad on a beach towel on the living room floor. Helen was whining about her life through bites, and idealizing her parents:

"You and Mom seemed so right to me. All Amos and I do is bicker."

"That can't be all."

"No. We take care of the kids, make dinners, watch TV shows, go to movies. We invite friends in, we—"

"All that. It's all silly. But lots of 'we' there, if I get to play the English teacher now that your mom isn't around. I don't know beans about much, but that 'we' hits the mark."

"The mark? Come on, Dad!"

"Come on yourself. The mark, the target, the point, the way 'we' stay 'we.'"

He stopped then, looking up at the ceiling for something more to say.

"I loved your mother like a tree loves the ground it's in: deep. But also almost, I think, without decision, where the seed falls in the wind. There was nothing wrong with that, especially when the ground was someone like Edie. But Amos is more interesting than me, more greedy to find something, or do something with his life. And so are you— and that makes things more complicated than your mom and me. Because basically I didn't care much, you see? I loved to teach, I spent my time teaching, I walked into this wonderful, ready-made family, I found you, and I found your mom. I found someone who wanted me and trusted me and didn't laugh at me too much and needed someone just like me around to take care of and to take care of her. And your mom loved teaching, and being a mom, and loving me and you and your kids and being loved by all of us. And she didn't seem to need much more than that—an adrenalin shot of travel, art, Kitty's adventure stories when she swept into town. Your mom and me, we just got lucky. And even if I didn't quite know it to say so, eventually I got it that it didn't get better than this."

He paused then.

"Didn't get any better, and didn't have to. There just wasn't any better to get."

"But I don't have that whatever it is you're talking about. That sense that he's there taking care of me and me of him."

"Probably not. And won't for a while. Or maybe you don't know what you have yet? Maybe you won't have it, the way your mom and I did. You're not your mom, who knew what she wanted and needed and got it and gave it. Edie seldom strayed from her own clear directions, her little sayings, even when life pushed her out of that territory. You're you, and you're stuck with you. Stuck where you get stuck, not where she did. And Amos is Amos, so he asks things of you I never needed or at least thought I never needed from your mom."

That quieted Helen for a few moments. Then she got up to finish her packing, giving Will a hug before she started collecting the paper plates and pizza box for the garbage. As she came back through the living room, heading to the hallway, she stopped and turned.

"One thing. You're wrong about the interesting. Oh, I know I idealize you and Mom too much. Maybe you're right, and I do need to think about what's there in the spats for me and what I get from helping Amos.

"But don't sell yourself short. All this that you've done: all this craziness, this painting, this mess, even her." Helen stopped then to point to the front door, closed now, no Nancy to see, though both of them saw her, as if she had more weight than all the piles of rocks that surrounded them.

"I think it's insane, Dad, all this stuff in the house. What you do with your time, these awful lines you've drawn all over the floor, these piles of yours, the paintings. But it is at least interesting. Mom would yell at you, or maybe laugh at you, but she'd know that too. Knew that, I bet, the minute she met you."

One more short pause, Helen looking down at the ground.

"Nancy knew it too. She told me a little about what happened to her: Jess leaving, her husband, the other guy in her life, coming here, that night."

Will looked up, surprised.

"Just a little. The stuff you wouldn't go into with me."

"It was her story, not mine."

"I don't care why, now. I did feel shut out, but you had your reasons, I guess."

She turned to look down at him, staring up at her from the towel that had been their tablecloth on the floor. She bent down, gave him a hug.

"Nancy said you took her in, made her know you liked her. 'That was a lot, you know,' she said to me. She remembered you a long time ago, when she was in your class and got pregnant and dropped out of school. 'Your dad and mom,' she told me. 'They talked to me, helped me get stuff from my locker. The kids and teachers and principal didn't want to get near me. Your mom gave me this little black journal and a pen, and your dad found some history book or other he hoped I might read. They didn't need to do that. Like Will didn't need to let me stay. But did.'"

Will smiled. "I forgot about that: the journal and history book."

"Of course you did. You just do what you do, Dad. Like Mom. That's what I mean. Even when you shut people out, you let them in."

He smiled, nodded his thanks, while Helen headed to her room. He got up eventually and stood in the doorway of the bedroom, looking at Helen kneeling on the mattress on the floor, until she looked back up at him.

"A couple years ago your mom woke me up to tell me this dream. She was on a mountain or some high peak and wanted to start down. There were other people with her, one of them me. We weren't ready to start down, or were arguing about something, or were ignoring her, so she just began going down the mountain without us, assuming we'd follow. She got on this narrow trail, I remember her calling it perilous, and repeating the word. But gradually—she repeated that word a lot too—gradually she made it most of the way down, until she came to these telephone booths. Then she noticed that we hadn't followed her and, even though she'd decided to leave us, she was upset at us for not coming after her. So she went into one of the booths and called back up to where we were, or where she thought we were.

"By that time, we'd left, she was told by someone who answered the phone, and we'd left in a different direction, since we had no idea where she'd gone. The person somehow knew this—that we'd given up trying to figure out where she went. This made her even angrier, though she realized that she'd been the one to leave.

"Then she woke up, annoyed. Put out enough that she woke me up to tell me the dream, accused me of abandoning her to argue and go off with these other people. And that left her on this perilous path. So even though she got where she needed to go, she was alone, calling back trying to figure out when we'd show up, and disappointed that we—or I—never did.

"She wasn't too sick then, that night. Or was, but we didn't know how sick yet, or didn't believe it and still thought she'd get better. At least I did. After she died, I remembered her telling me this story, and I started wondering if the dream really was about what it means to be alone. I started seeing it in terms of disease, or death, or the way people just get tired of each other after long lifetimes together, worn down by the little rubbings of shoulders and habits. Or simply they just go off, no reason, and then they can't go back, or don't want to, or want to but there's nothing to go back to, no one to answer the phone.

"So that was my version of the dream. But in the last few months, living alone myself, I stopped putting myself into this story. I realized I stopped caring who was on top of the mountain, who on the bottom, with or without whoever else, or what way they came down. I was just interested in the trail. Edie didn't tell me much about the trail, except that it was perilous, and she needed to travel it gradually. But that's where I'd go if I could get into that dream myself: onto that trail, working my way down, curious to see what there was to see, careful where I put my feet."

Helen waited a moment before asking:

"And the telephone booths? Who would you call?"

"You mean the ones I left or thought left me? And were arguing with? I haven't gotten there. To the booth. That's for later."

"You've got your rocks instead."

He smiled at that.

"Yes. My rocks. I guess they're my trail. Or I call them, all the time."

"Get any answers?"

He looked at his daughter then, thankful she was willing to enter his fantasy.

"Can't say, yet," Will responded. And then added, after a pause, "But they do keep me asking questions."

Then Will went over and kissed Helen's forehead as she knelt there, packing away her clothes for her return home.

As he left the room, he stopped and turned back. "I'm selling myself short. I can say. No answers. The trail, the phone booth. Someone to call. It's a lot, enough."

161

"You are a little crazy, you know," Helen told her father, who smiled back at her, as if that was the most obvious thing in the world.

Will stood a moment longer watching Helen, then walked down the hall, and out the door into the early evening light. The walk took him to the beach, and from there he wandered along the coast, turning inland to one street after another, heading vaguely south. He eventually realized he was moving toward Nancy's home, or former home, and let himself increase his pace, in her honor. When he got to the little park, he stopped, settled down on the ground under his usual cypress, and looked across the grassy knoll to the empty windows. They were draped now. There were no cars in the driveway. There was nothing there, really—just a handsome split-level ranch house that was a little newer, a little bigger, and a little fancier than its neighbors. A little more secretive. Dangerous, Will thought to himself, and then corrected that idea: he couldn't be sure. So he just sat, watched a few families struggle carrying chairs and coolers and other paraphernalia up from the entrance to the beach behind him, saw a mother pull her baby from its stroller to comfort its crying, heard cars along the narrow streets. Then he got up and went home to his paints, his daughter, his cat, and his loneliness.

7

REVOLVING WOMEN, WILL SAID TO HIMSELF, when Kitty called to announce her arrival the day after he kissed Helen good-bye. He expected this exchange—even looked forward to it. Helen left with an assortment of small presents for her children, a hug and thanks to her father, and the promise from him that he would visit early in the fall. With that promise came hers to leave him alone for the next few weeks. Will found himself relieved by her trust, and sadder than he expected as he walked through the house he once again could call his own, eerily quiet after his recent visitors.

He opened the door eagerly for Kitty when she knocked. Along with her energy, she brought him two metal pieces that she and Benny made in the studio of the New Mexico artist she wrote him about. Benny's construction consisted of two wide, trapezoidal appendages—bat wings, Will quickly understood—with a pencil-thin bit of metal between marked by a quite large asymmetrical head that hung below the plane of the wings and body; rough letters across the width of the sculpture spelled "TOT" in large bright red. Kitty's was more elaborate: a series of angular arcs and planes that created a semblance of a face—small nose, jutting chin, narrow cheeks that triangulated to a striated arc to form a representation of a receding hairline. Below the nose, the mouth had been replaced by a small wood-handled paint brush that was hooked into the metal by two protruding edges he took for teeth; the brush itself extended horizontally out from the facial structure on both ends.

Will placed both pieces affectionately onto the mantel, hiding how the gifts moved him as Kitty related details of how each was constructed, and as he introduced her to Scotty, peeking shyly from the hallway at the two of them. He asked about Benny, was told the boy was back with his parents, who were back with each other and back in California, nearby enough that she expected to see him often. Will was promised, or warned, to expect the boy some weekend soon.

He and Kitty went for a walk by the ocean. The sun was still out when they arrived, but they could see the fog pushing in rapidly across the water. In ten minutes they were covered in its soft white chill. When Kitty started to question him, Will was not surprised that she seemed already in possession of more facts or presumptions about his time with Nancy than he'd been willing to supply when they talked on the phone.

"You've been busy," she started.

He looked at her shyly.

"I guess so. Things keep happening, that's for sure."

She laughed. "It's Mr. Passive Voice himself. Things keep happening? Because of other people, right? You're just painting rocks."

He pretended he didn't notice her annoyance.

"When I find the time."

"What with the intrusions, obstacles that people have set up in your way, right? Mob scene between you and your easel."

"Only takes one or two. People, that is. Sometimes just their memory."

"Edie's didn't seem to stop you. Did Nancy's? Or no, Nancy wasn't a memory, was she? Or not just?"

He stopped walking then, looked away from her to the water, still visible through the fog, and let a couple with a small dog pass them on the left, a bicyclist zip by on the right. He wanted to dismiss Kitty's challenges as a desire to simplify, but that didn't wash. He had to admit to himself that he counted on Kitty's doggedness to help him see his way through his convenient, prickly bushes of self-deception.

"Is there something you want to know?"

"Details about you and her, you mean? Of course. But those can wait. For now: why?"

"Why what?"

"Why all of it? The rocks still, but mostly the woman, the Nancy. Right? That's her name? That you stared at nights when you told me you were walking around aimlessly? And the fire, and her son who you got to know and you also never told me about. Why? What are you after? Where are you going? Do you have any idea what's happening? Why it's happening? What you want? You spend months keeping me at arm's length—arm's? no, wooden beams, pole vault lengths—and then you wind up shacking up with someone you see through a window at night?"

"You think I've done something wrong?"

"You can be so deliberately stupid when you want to, Will. I'm not your moral radar. I'm the flake, right? The one who screws her way around the world, hires hunks to work in her garden so she can watch the sweat shine on their six-packs? Don't turn me into your conscience now just because I'm asking you to think about what you're doing."

"So tell me."

"I don't know or I wouldn't be asking. You teach for what—two, three decades? You love this woman almost as long, marry her, care for her 'til death do you part. Learn to care for her friend you never even liked much for a long time. (Yes, I know that too.) And suddenly, in months, or weeks, you throw all that over, turn your living room into a cave, start collecting trash before the garbage men can get to it, go peeping through windows ..."

She paused, out of breath.

"Anything I've left out?"

"Only the painting."

"Right, the painting. And the rocks and driftwood. How could I forget?"

He chimed in himself then.

"And the walls covered with Masonite on wires. And the floor covered with footprints and smudges. And the shed gone."

"Good. Now my turn again. Staring at a woman, hours at a time, through rain and sleet, cold and fog. But that's not enough for Mr. Widow over here. So you take the woman into your house, let her husband beat you up, burn down your shed."

At that point, Will felt he'd let Kitty play long enough. He put his hand up to Kitty's mouth, gently, but firmly.

"Stop, Kitty. I know what I've done, what I haven't done, who I've been. No need to repeat more of it."

"You sure, Will? Then tell me why. You're the one who teaches kids to be suspicious of reading good motives into history, who wants them thinking no one's innocent and good intentions can kill as surely as bombs or the need for revenge."

"You've been listening all these years."

"Don't change the subject. But yes. That's how much you know, or want to know, about me."

She paused then, maybe just to catch her breath, maybe because of the smile she saw on his face. She reached into a pocket, fumbled for her sunglasses, put them on. Then realized she wasn't quite done.

"I guess that's part of it, Will. The way you've treated me. Or ignored and patronized me for so long. I noticed. I cared, more now than ever. You can be a prick, you know that? Just by being nice sometimes, the way you are nice. Polite as the salesman at the door. And if you know so little after so long about me, someone you've known forever, what the hell do you think you know about this Nancy and her husband and her kid—these total strangers?"

"I don't know squat. You're right about that. I don't know anything about any of them. I suppose I owe you half a lifetime of apologies. But they're not quite strangers. She was a student years ago. I taught her sons."

"Oh, of course. Now it all makes sense."

He thought it did in some odd way. He was once their teacher; he shared some nights in the rain and chill with one, watching the other. And here he was. Simple as that. Or almost.

He wasn't, he decided suddenly, ready to explain much more—to Kitty any more than to Helen or Nancy. Or anyone else. Except maybe Edie, who didn't seem to be asking.

But Kitty's outburst confirmed what Will had been thinking.

He took Kitty's elbow, turning her in the direction of a stairway that led down to the beach below the small lighthouse that the city had reclaimed as a surfing museum. Between navigating the narrow concrete stairs and Kitty slipping out of socks and new pale blue sneakers once they got down to the sand, he bought himself a few minutes before deciding what to say next.

"Edie gave me to you, didn't she? Or begged you to take me."

When Kitty turned her face away from him, he knew he'd guessed right. It was what he'd been wondering ever since Helen had slipped with her comment when she walked into the living room. Helen and Kitty, he was sure, were colluding all these months.

"You're crazy. And avoiding my questions."

"Guilty no doubt of both," Will conceded. "But no more secrets. Please. You know what I'm asking. Something happened with the two of you, you and Edie, didn't it? Before you left. Before she died. She said something, or wrote it, or just talked it with those eyes of hers. About taking care of me, watching over me, taking me over."

Kitty didn't answer for a moment, while she stared over his shoulder down the sand.

"We talked about everything, Will. Don't be vain enough to think we spent our time on you."

"I'm sure you didn't. Not all your time. But there was something. Did she know about the two of us?"

"Of course not."

"I don't mean did you tell her. I'm asking if she knew. I didn't think she did, not until the last couple weeks. But now I do."

"What's made you change your mind?"

"You and Helen. The pen you've been keeping me in. It all fits somehow: Helen barging in wanting to help or asking for help—expecting to find Nancy around, checking up on Dad, now you showing up when you have, right after Nancy leaves, right after Helen."

"You are a child of the '60s, conspiracy theories and all."

"Now you're patronizing me. You're hiding something, I know that. What did Edie put you up to? I know you'd do anything for her if she asked."

Kitty started to say something quickly but Will stopped her; stopped her mouth again with his hand, shook his head at her while he moved his other hand to her shoulder and then gently to the sides of her face, insisting she look at him. It was a quiet stretch of beach. He could see some surfers in the water, people walking at

169

the edge of his vision. A pair of towels held in place by a backpack flapped against the ridge behind the two of them.

"Stop. It's time to tell me. Please."

She did stop—stopped struggling to move out of his grasp, stopped trying to look away from him out to the water, stopped smiling that grim angry smile she'd held to all the time they'd been talking. Instead, she looked at him, quietly, sadly. Lovingly, Will realized, letting himself see her for who she was.

He released his grip on her face. She seemed to shrink, or settle, let herself diminish in size as she sighed, stared off to the water, turned back to him, then looked down to her toes, driving them fiercely into the dry warm sand. She started to cry—slowly, softly—while he waited, as quiet in himself as he had been in weeks, maybe months.

"Yes. She asked me to take care of you, watch out for you, whatever you want to call it. I don't know if she knew about us. She'd never say if she did, you know that. Maybe. It doesn't matter, or I don't think it matters. Or didn't anyway, then. But she knew how much I loved her, and loved you. I mean really loved you, came to, over these years."

She turned her face off to the ocean with that confession. And went on, hurriedly.

"And since she's died, I've come to think Edie knew I needed something else in my life besides home decoration. I don't know what she knew. All she said was, 'Watch him,' in that hoarse whisper of hers. That was all, Will. Just that, that—what can I call it? Instruction. And just once. No details, no 'please,' nothing else. A little bit of a smile when I nodded my head, which I took as thank you. That was it. She didn't hand you over or tell me what to do. You are right: I'd do pretty much anything for Edie. But not anything, not everything. Even I have my limits. I promised to watch you. The rest is me. And you."

She held back before the last words, and they came out mumbled, as if she wanted to keep them under her tongue a little longer. But he heard them, touched his hand to her arm. Then he turned his eyes to the security of the water himself, as if trying to rearrange the sheets of his thoughts after a turbulent night.

"I miss her," was all he said when he turned back to Kitty.

"Me too," Kitty replied, looking up at him with a quiet sense of resignation in what had been restored between them, slipping her arm beneath his elbow as she turned him so they could continue to walk together down the empty stretch of sand.

•　　　•　　　•

Will and Kitty took up where they had left off two months earlier. Will returned to his painting, along with his late night walks, often ending them atop his roof, where he'd loiter for thirty minutes or more, staring out across the town, once even falling asleep there to awaken to bird calls and a stiff neck in the early morning. He didn't search garbage cans—Nancy had cured him of that. Instead, he was content to just walk through neighborhoods where he'd once loitered, confirming with a smile the ongoing consistency of bedtimes, dog barks, and movements of light in the houses. He would find his way to the beaches that lined the waterfront, scramble down via steps or rocks, and sit in the cold fog that enveloped the sand. He still carried his backpack, and would pick up stray bottles, bits of glass, abandoned plastic buckets and shovels, Frisbees, and other random finds along the way, which he'd dump into a large cardboard box in his living room that Kitty called his "toy chest." The collection of discards would sit there awhile; maybe he'd set one or two of them up as part of a still life. Then one day he'd see the box empty, as Kitty decided it was time to drop off the contents at Goodwill. He didn't protest her decisions, nor help her carry the stuff out to her car.

July 7.

Thinginess. Presence. Not the same I'm thinking.

Thinginess, that three-dimensional-ishness, is our way to confirm the world's weight. Its thereness, hereness. And ours. This is a rock, this a bottle. This is me, you. (Always me, you, that insane, repeated need for rediscovery.)

Presence is something else. Here and gone, thing and not. Kitty here, gone, yet here. Edie gone and ghostly but all over, my air.

Real painters seem to start with thinginess? Then teach us how thin it can get and still be? Or maybe stop being only a thing, and become presence?

So I think, today.

Will and Kitty had one small conversation that hinted at all the others they were avoiding when she suggested he sand the floors to remove the paint smudges and foot patterns that covered the living room.

"You want to remodel my house for me, Kitty? Not enough projects to busy yourself with? This one can wait, I think."

"Wait? Ah, that sounds ominous, like you're making plans, thinking about the future. More, more."

"No plans. Wait means not now. It doesn't mean then. You sound like Helen. I think the floors bothered her more than anything while she was here."

"The conspiracy of women rears its ugly head once again. OK. Drop the sanding; keep the paint blobs and shoe prints. How about a new shirt? Yours looks diseased."

He had to admit that he was tired of the few he wore and rewore all year, until now they were thin, saggy, encrusted with his paint.

"Maybe a shirt."

"Or two?"

"Or two. Sure."

"Good."

She paused for a moment before continuing.

"I was thinking of slowing down, making a habit of you if you could stand it."

He liked that, her moving less, maybe him moving a little more. He nodded, smiled at her.

She spoke into his silence. "If I'm going to be around, I'd like to sit somewhere."

"Now you do sound like Helen. Pillows aren't enough?"

"Why not waterbeds and beanbag chairs? Some madras bedspreads over the windows? A little patchouli incense in the corner to go with Janis Joplin 45s?"

"Mmm."

"Mmm yourself. Why not admit you're not who you were when you made all this—last fall or whenever it was—not even who you were when I found you in … when was it? February?"

Will stopped his painting and turned to her, not sure what he wanted to admit.

"Agreed for the moment," he said. "Now what?"

"Exactly," Kitty all but shouted. "Exactly. Now what? If you want, we could find out."

He smiled at her challenge, or offer, whatever it was, taken aback and pushed beyond comfort by her earnestness. But he wasn't ready, he felt. Was sure. Not for a "we"—this one, anyway.

So he stalled.

"I'm not different enough yet to give all this up, Kitty. Or this is how I'm different so it's not something I'm going to give up."

He was pleased with his answer—proud of it even—and he wondered thinking back to the moment that night if he might even have had a self-satisfied grin on his face.

Kitty looked at him, deciding (it seemed to him) among anger, exasperation, or defeat. She laughed.

"OK. For now, I'll put my director's chair back in the car. But get your hat and your wallet. Two shirts for you, then lunch. I'm hungry, you're buying."

He was hungry too, he realized, looking at the pale cerulean blue and raw sienna that sat along his fingers, smeared together like a thin veil over the tiny brown spots that were slowly taking over his pale flesh. Thinking he needed to wash before they left. Thinking again, that he didn't, or didn't want to bother. Instead he swiped at his hand with his color-stained rag, then used the same rag on the brush he held before he dropped it, unceremoniously, into the vat of dirty water.

July 13.

To make a place.
For myself.
Not for myself.
For not myself.
That would be something.

•   •   •

Kitty did stay, more or less, into August. She came over most afternoons, watched him paint, read her magazines, left, came back the next day. Weekends she'd arrive earlier, push him out with her to a round of garage sales and make him buy her lunch, then drop him off before heading wherever she headed, leaving him to wonder sometimes what he was missing by never asking if he could come along. For the most part, he was content not to know.

Benny visited her for two weeks while his parents went off to Mexico, and the three of them resumed the rhythms they had settled into with each other in the winter and spring: days at the house and wandering the beaches, the boy supplying interference for the two adults, still wary of each other in ways neither was ready to admit. Between them, Benny and Will continued to revisit Tot and his loyal friends, who had now discovered a passage deep in the cave that let them emerge almost anywhere on earth, though so far mostly confined in their wandering to adventures in

Boston and New Mexico, where Will could get Benny to help him invent new escapades. This way he learned about Benny's time watching the Red Sox; the bicycle his parents rented for him with training wheels that disappeared before the end of his visit; the Nuclear Science museum in Albuquerque (that sent chills down Will's anti-atomic skin). The Switcheroos were replaced by Yankees in pinstripes, ravens and mosquitoes, spies.

Alone other weeks, Will and Kitty walked along the ocean, or at a nearby park; sometimes holding hands, sometimes shoulder to shoulder along a railing looking down at the beach, or across to families on blankets in the grass. One weekend, she even managed to get him to sit with her by the water at a bar and watch the sunset. Another day, she forced him to take her to Nancy's old house, where the two sat beneath the tree and stared for a few moments before resuming their walk. He was surprised that she asked him nothing while they were there, or after—just sat beside him, silent, shifting her weight now and then. They moved back to their old ritual of welcoming and departing hugs. And stopped there.

Sometimes Kitty would be gone for a day or two without telling him beforehand, but she'd always show up again just when he thought to worry. He got several postcards from Nancy, settled ("for a while, anyway") in Austin in a small studio apartment a short walk from her father's house ("near enough that I can occasionally make dinner for the boys, far enough that they can live with that"), with a job at a law firm ("a couple people here do good work with immigrants, which pays for the crap drug cases that buy them their Rolexes"). He missed her at night in bed, but even more he missed the quiet ease of their meshed schedules, the simple complicity they'd fallen into so easily. He'd never quite had that with anyone. Even Edie, he realized. He took some comfort in Scotty, who had that same quiet indifference to or acceptance of his environment that Nancy displayed, relishing Kitty's attentive petting when she was around, steadfast at her nighttime post at the foot of Will's mattress.

His painting didn't get much better, but he stopped worrying about that fact. Looking back at some of the photographs of his earlier efforts, he did think he saw change, a difference.

Kitty told him in passing one day that his paintings looked "less cluttered."

"You're using fewer rocks, letting space in more, keeping up a better perspective, letting the objects bustle about with each other. The way I've long told you one has to for a room to show its personality."

Will couldn't quite see all that, but he let himself be content in her analysis.

He started a new series—his first without rocks—of large-scale paintings of small objects: some broken bottles and cups, a cracked inkwell, matches, candles, thimbles, paperclips, tacks. He realized with a start that this is where he'd more or less begun last fall, with his small pebbles. It was easier now, he thought. He could, a little, account for size, change proportions, notice the small gradations in his little toys. But by and large the results were as undistinguished as all his painting.

Still, Kitty noticed, and vocalized, the change one day in her way.

"You're moving forward."

"There's direction? You think this is progress?"

"It's a step up from the rocks, I'd say. More homey."

"Rocks last longer. The bottles are broken, the pitchers shattered, the metal stuff rusted. This little shit gets lost faster than one of Benny's toys."

"But you found them in the first place."

"Yeah. I suppose. I found the rocks too."

"But you don't matter to the rocks. Rocks aren't lost. They're there whether you found them or not. The bottles and thimble aren't."

"Hmmm."

"Then tell me why you tried to help Nancy."

"You're good," he said to her with a smile. "I just did it. That's what people do. Useless things because they're useless."

"Hmmm."

Will looked at her, but her head was already sunk back down into her magazine, as if she hadn't broken her attention for a moment. He continued to look a little longer than usual, as a painter might. Thinking how he'd mix some alizarin crimson into wet ochre for the spread of her cheeks, muss the edge of the small footballs of her eyes with diluted Payne's gray for the dark spread of shadow at the corners, maybe smudge some darkened violet to create the underside of her face bones as they rounded down into her cleft chin.

It would be interesting, he thought, to try to paint her sometime, let her sit and notice me noticing her while she remained still if not quiet. He pictured her relishing the sustained attention, if more than a little surprised by how embarrassed she felt under his gaze after waiting for it so

178

long; nervous despite herself to see what he'd make of her, what she'd look like; uncomfortable at this awkward position of being the done to rather than the doer.

In the meantime, they wrestled over ideas. There was the day, for example, when she walked in and saw his notebook open on the counter. The last line he had written was a quotation: *From a few things, to get everything.*

She walked to the living room, carrying the open notebook, until he noticed, politely took it from her, and closed it.

"'Everything from a few things.' Nice line. Yours?"

"Now it is. From a catalogue somewhere. Sounds right."

"Sounds like something to hang over the mantel. Embroider on your pillowcases."

"Or try to remember," Will answered, refusing to be won over by her cynicism.

"Have you?" she asked.

"Have I what?"

"Gotten everything. From your few things."

"Some. A little. Enough, I think."

"Enough for what?"

Will took her question seriously, paused to think through his answer: "Enough to get me up in the morning."

He paused then, laughed.

"More. For here you are, you and Benny. Helen."

"And Nancy, and Jess."

"Yes, them too. Isn't that almost everything?"

"Cute. Yes. Here we are. But we're not, I'm certainly not, one of your few things."

"No, I suppose not. Of course yes too."

Then it was Kitty's turn to pause, take a moment to look at what Will was proposing, rather than push back with her usual annoyance.

"Your yeses and noes; your maybe thises and maybe thats. You stuff a lot into what you call your few things."

Will smiled, though he hid his pleasure by keeping his own face turned toward his work, an awkward reproduction of two bottles, a coffee can, and a small black packing box.

July 25

To want to feel again.
How good that feels.

•   •   •

Things came to a head between them over wisteria vines. Will brought them up, late one August afternoon when they were in their usual positions—he at his canvases, she at her magazines. They were back from a morning of garage sales, a walk along the ocean, and a lunch of burritos eaten on a bench overlooking a beach full of bright towels, sand castles, crying children, and sunburned backs. The beach scene had them arguing about beauty: if there was any, what it was, whether he appreciated it "when you lock yourself away from daylight to paint" (her challenge to him), whether she did when she ran around the world after knickknacks she could offer her customers as "profiteering substitutes for sensation" (his challenge to her). He insisted that all he did with his colors was try to track light; she that she brought lusciousness into cold homes. He must have gotten under her skin, though, because, after a short silence while he munched at his food and she looked out to sea, she turned on him.

"You don't even seem hungry when you eat. You don't salivate enough. Drip some spittle on one of your precious paintings sometime, Will, and see what happens."

He laughed, but was hurt. As they drove back to his house, they went past the high school, where he glanced up at his old classroom window, then across the street to the wisteria vine on the corner house that he used to stare at for minutes at a time. Later, as he stood at his painting, he found himself returning to their argument. His voice came out thicker and angrier than he expected when he started to speak.

"You really pissed me off this afternoon, you know. With your talk about what I don't see. Let me tell you something I do see."

She looked up from her reading.

"Across from the high school are these simple fences: thick stocky poles—maybe waist high—and wide squares of strong wire. They're there to hold up the old wisteria vines that grow along the edge of the corner house. One of the oldest vines in town, I think; you must know it with all your damn garden tours."

"Of course. They're famous."

"Whatever. Do you and your gardener friends ever look at the vines themselves, not the flowers? There's all that teeming life of the things when they're in bloom, I'm sure it's quite beautiful. But the vines themselves—the vines, that's what's great to me. I would look at them, flowers or not, all year from my classroom window. The flowers would come and go, but the vines stayed put; just got bigger and thicker over the years. They're like tree trunks: wide, twisted. They are really the fence for that house, not the wire and wood they agree to grow along. The wire and wood are there just to give them a path for their wandering."

Kitty was surprised enough by Will's vehemence to pause for a minute before answering.

"There's a moral here, right, Will? Something I'm supposed to learn? Something I'm supposed to be dumb about because all I see are the flowers? And all I smell is the tangle of spring that gets so strong sometimes it must have even gotten to some of your students sitting there doodling their way through your lectures on whatever you get to by April and May—the New Deal? Cold War? Commies and the Fellow Travelers? Eisenhower White House?"

"Usually the New Frontier, Vietnam, sit-ins. Civil rights and the riots."

"Tear gas and wisteria. That's nice."

Will looked at her to see whether her archness was as annoyed as it sounded. Only mildly bemused, he thought, she staring at him over the rim of her reading glasses and the top edge of an *Architectural Digest* featuring a prize-winning kitchen remodel on the cover.

"Forget the moral. Or mostly. I think what I was getting at was something about how all we should be doing is playing fence to vines, sort of like poles for the peas to climb, instead of always taking charge, always wanting to be the peas, the flowers, the bloom, the bright colors, the show. Just notice the vines next time."

"I always have, you insulting ass. There's that strange shaggy look to them that only old wisteria has, like the wood's shedding, losing dry skin, starting over again and again. Only the shagginess never really goes away, the shagginess really is the skin, old and new, joined and distinct."

She stopped for a second.

"Separate, but equal, I'd call them, if I were a smart historian like you."

He looked at her in surprise—that surprise he always felt inside his shame as he once again underestimated someone. He hid it by turning back to his painting.

But Kitty wasn't done.

"So since you're so determined to be my teacher: what is it I'm missing, that matters so much to you?"

This time he was the one who paused, long enough to put down his paintbrush and look up from the still life to the two metal sculptures from Kitty and Benny sitting on the mantel.

"When I was teaching, I kept looking out at them, at the vines, thinking how the fence was just there to let the plants wend their way, to keep them up and shaped, but not quite tame. That's the way I felt about my life with Edie most of the time."

He turned to Kitty then, saw her looking directly at him, the magazine closed on her lap.

"That's what I thought my job was, just to be there to let Edie and Helen grow, thick and shaggy and solid, spreading themselves out into the world in their own ways."

"While you stood around, strong and upright, staunch and forgotten amid the flowers, a convenient bunch of wire and wood."

"I guess. I never thought of it like that. I thought of what it felt like to have all that vine around me, year after year, spreading out in its own ways. Its own wonderful ways, so quiet and so full. And I had my classes, you know, where I got more adoration than I knew what to do with, when I needed attention."

"Oh, I'm not talking about admirers, Will. That's too easy. I'm talking about growing and flowering."

He had to face her earnestness for a moment, before he laughed and turned back to his painting.

"You've been to too many actualizing retreats, Kitty. Your brain's gone soft."

"No, it's my heart that's softened, however you want to try to laugh your way out of my love."

He didn't try. Or at least he didn't try to laugh. He just looked up from his painting to the two gifts there on the mantel, then let his gaze spread along the wall to the row on row of still lifes. Finally, he turned his head to look at her, sitting on her director's chair in the corner of his living room, staring back at him. He tried to figure out what to do now that she had once again breached the wall, crossed this line they had both drawn—or at least both respected—for the last long months. The smile he offered her was all he could find inside himself to smudge that line, before turning back to his painting.

Kitty stared at him a few more seconds. From the corner of his eye, fiercely avoiding eye contact, he watched her shake her head slowly from side to side, lower her chin to stare at the magazine in her lap, look up at the ceiling for a few moments, back to him, and finally back to the magazine on her lap. Then he saw her shift in her chair, bend down, collect the magazines she had scattered around her. She stood, folded her chair, leaned it against a wall, walked over to him, kissed him lightly on the cheek. Then, quiet still, she turned, assembled her things, and let herself out the door while he stood, immobile, pretending he was not watching her go.

•   •   •

It took him a week to call her. Her answering machine told the world that she had left town and would be back in a month or so. At the end of that message was a private note: "Will, if you call: I've kept my promise. Now I have other promises to keep."

He tried her cell, got the same messages public and private, left a message there for her: "No more about promises. Please call."

When she finally did, three weeks after that, it was already mid-September. She was home again. Just for a few days, she said. What did he want?

He wanted to invite her for dinner. He went shopping for salmon, salad, white wine, ice cream, another new shirt, beige slacks, two plates, candles and candleholders, silverware, cloth napkins. And two sturdy wooden chairs, that he set around the dining room table, now restored to its old position in the dining room itself. He put on the shirt, pants, and clean socks. She came over in a simple black dress cut at the knee, in stockings and short heels. He hadn't seen her in anything but jeans and slacks the past months.

"Those small piles of rocks along the front path," she asked at the door. "Cairns?"

He smiled, nodded his head, glad she got his little joke. "For you, in case you lose the way."

"Never have before. Coming to see you anyway. Maybe for you, in case you forget how to get home?"

"Maybe." He nodded his concession. Then he paused for a moment. "Or just to get a few of the rocks out of the house. See how else they can serve me."

He lifted a worn hand, clearly washed but still grimy with paint to her cheek and rubbed it there for a moment.

"Thank you for coming," he said.

"Don't thank me yet. I'm just hungry, like I always am, and you promised me dinner."

She looked beyond him to the window, where late afternoon sun was fighting to sustain itself for a few more minutes before the night fog took over. The tarp was gone; the floor cleaned—though covered still with faint smudges of pencil and paint. The blinds were open.

"You've discovered sunshine."

"Seems so."

He dropped his hand from her cheek and turned to look out the living room windows with her.

"Glad to see you've accepted light."

"I've always accepted light. Always. That's what I've been tracking all this time, don't you know?"

"Ahh, tracking. Historian's word. Pretending there are patterns. To time, light, life."

"Mmm."

"Mmm yourself. Cezanne said there are no lines, no designs, color made them all. Just reds and yellows and blues."

"And that's all?"

"Isn't it enough? Some dabs of a this and dabs of a that and dabs of an other. No tracks; just mixes, variations."

"I'll get back to you on that."

She laughed at him, shaking her head at his refusal to let go of consistency.

"You know people can see in now, peek at you the way you peek at other people. Make you into the one to spy on at night."

"There's nothing to see."

"Really?"

He looked around himself then, at the oddness, at the emptiness, imagining what he would have thought of a space like this a year ago.

"Yes, really."

Kitty turned away from the window to his easel.

"And you've discovered fruit. And watercolors."

She walked by him to the assortment of apples, oranges, tomatoes, and bananas sitting on a small wooden table where the dining room one had been.

He smiled, though not wide enough to let her notice the effect of her attention.

"More portable, the watercolors. Started going outside a little to paint in the daytime."

"And the bananas, apples, tomatoes?"

"Wanted to try something new."

"Careful, they're perishable."

"I noticed that. Hard to keep up with those spots on bananas. Skins a bitch to get right."

"Get right?"

"If things change, you want to get them right, don't you?"

"I don't know. If things change, my tendency is just to try to keep up."

"Isn't that the same?"

"As right? I don't think so. I'm just trying to stay in step, not pretend I know the score. But I like that, working with things that rot."

"Not because they rot."

"No, because they might, Will, if you don't eat them." Then she added, "Whatever your motives, this is promising."

He paused for a minute, ready to stop talking in code. "Sorry," he said next, turning away from his canvases, his still life, and his colors to face her. "And done with promises. Really. Promise."

He smiled then, moved his hand back to her cheek, then around her face to her hair, pushing his fingers into the dense black thickness of it.

She raised her hand to cover his, pull it away to her lips, rubbing her face and fingers over the coarse sandy terrain of him for a moment before moving in closer.

"It's about time!" she exclaimed, brushing her lips up against his mouth for a second before standing back and starting to push him, half-angrily, backwards through the narrow path of the living room, past his picture wall and his stacks of rocks and bottles, past his toy chest and his spattered floorboards.

She kept pushing, while he moved slowly and tentatively backwards step by step, into the hallway, trying not to turn, trying to trust her to provide direction, leaning slightly into her so her fingers strained against his chest. She was strong, he remembered that now, from their few nights together. Willful. Domineering even. And so was he—he remembered that too, that odd spirit in him that came out those nights.

Then he was at the bedroom door and through it. He felt the baseboard of the bed behind him, just above the knees, then felt himself buckle, fall, tumble back onto the mattress. Kitty fell on top of him.

They didn't use the chairs that night or the nights that followed, but ate, when they did, sitting up in bed, naked or nearly so, not talking much, as quiet with each other as two lifelong friends could be who didn't know what came next.

ABOUT THE AUTHOR

Paul Skenazy grew up in Chicago and studied at the University of Chicago and Stanford University. He taught literature and writing for thirty-five years at the University of California, Santa Cruz. His nonfiction works include a book on James M. Cain, a collection of essays on place in San Francisco literature, and a selection of interviews with Maxine Hong Kingston. He has published more than three hundred reviews of fiction and nonfiction for newspapers and magazines nationwide, and was twice nominated for the National Book Critics Circle award for reviewing. For a dozen years, he was a mystery review columnist for the *Washington Post*.

His short novel *Temper CA* (2019) won the Miami University Press Novella Contest. He revised and edited *La Mollie and the King of Tears* (1996), a posthumous novel by Arturo Islas, and his autobiographical piece on Chicago and Saul Bellow was a "Notable" essay in *The Best American Essays, 2015*. Stories and essays have recently appeared in *Catamaran Literary Reader*, *Chicago Quarterly Review*, and elsewhere. He lives in Santa Cruz, California, with his wife, the poet Farnaz Fatemi.

You Might Also Enjoy

PIOUS REBEL

by Jory Post

After her partner dies suddenly, Lisa Hardrock realizes how little she knows about the life she's been living — and starts exploring her questions in a blog that unexpectedly goes viral.

Smith: An Unauthorized Fictography

by Jory Post

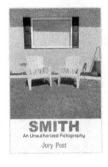

In this kaleidoscopic, episodic joy ride of thirty interviews that may or may not be real, all of them in conversation with an interviewer who is herself a mystery.

Available from Paper Angel Press in
hardcover, trade paperback, and digital editions
paperangelpress.com